The
Astonishing
maybe

The Astonishing maybe

Shaunta Grimes

FEIWEL AND FRIENDS
NEW YORK

A FEIWEL AND FRIENDS BOOK

An imprint of Macmillan Publishing Group, LLC

175 Fifth Avenue, New York, NY 10010

Our books may be purchased in bulk for promotional, educational, or business use.
Please contact your local bookseller or the Macmillan Corporate
and Premium Sales Department at (800) 221-7945 ext. 5442 or by e-mail at
MacmillanSpecialMarkets@macmillan.com.

Library of Congress Cataloging-in-Publication Data

Names: Grimes, Shaunta, author.

Title: The astonishing maybe / Shaunta Grimes.

Description: First edition. | New York : Feiwel and Friends, [2019]

Identifiers: LCCN 2018019103| ISBN 9781250191830 (hardcover) |
    ISBN 9781250191847 (eBook)

Subjects: | CYAC: Soon after his family's move to small-town Nevada, rising Seventh
    grader Gideon befriends an intriguing neighbor, Rooney, who is hiding secrets about
    her past. | Friendship—Fiction. | Neighbors—Fiction. | Family problems—Fiction. |
    Moving, Household—Fiction. | Family life—Nevada—Fiction. | Nevada—Fiction.

Classification: LCC PZ7.1.G7545 Ast 2019 | DDC [Fic]—dc23

LC record available at https://lccn.loc.gov/2018019103

Book design by Carol Ly

Feiwel and Friends logo designed by Filomena Tuosto

First edition, 2019

1 3 5 7 9 10 8 6 4 2

mackids.com

For my Wonder Roo

One

About halfway through Tennessee, I decided that I would never, not ever, forgive my parents for dragging me to live in some dirt town in rural Nevada.

"Not Nev-*ah*-da. Nev-a-da. A-like-in-apple right in the middle. Better learn to pronounce it like a native," Dad said for about the millionth time, "or they'll make you move to California."

Whatever. I didn't want to be a native of Nev-a-da or Nev-*ah*-da or anywhere but Wildwood, New Jer-sey. "At least California has an ocean."

"Are we going to the beach?" my little sister, Harper, asked. "I want to go to the beach."

"Yeah, right," I said. "We're never going to the beach again. We're moving to the desert."

"You're pouting so hard, I can *hear* it, Gideon." Dad tilted the rearview mirror so he saw me through it. I barely suppressed the urge to stick out my tongue.

"So, will we be in Tennessee forever or what?" I asked.

"Would you like to be?" He flicked on the blinker and slowed, swerving toward the shoulder. "I mean, it wouldn't be *my* first choice, but . . ."

I scrunched in my seat, arms crossed over my chest. "No."

"You're sure?" Mom turned in her seat and looked at me. "I hear Nashville's real nice."

I was tempted to call her bluff and say *yes, leave me in Tennessee*. Mom wouldn't even let me go to the boardwalk with my friends without making an adult cross their heart and hope to die that they wouldn't leave us alone.

Dad clucked his tongue against his teeth. "I have a job all lined up in Logandale. Nashville's out for me. But I bet we could find a circus around here somewhere that would pay good money for you, if your heart's set on staying in Tennessee forever."

"Dad!"

"So"—he stuck out his bottom lip and lifted one shoulder like it didn't matter to him one way or the other—"you want to keep going?"

"Yes."

"Right-o, Boss." He shot me a little salute and somehow turned things around so that continuing this drive west in an SUV pulling a trailer full of our stuff was *my* idea.

Harper leaned forward in her booster seat and said, "Hey, Giddy's not the boss. I'm the boss!"

"Don't call me Giddy," I said.

Harper bounced in her seat. "Giddyup! Giddy-up!"

"Mommmm!"

Mom said, "Okay, Harper. That's enough now."

I turned my scowl out the window and waited to get to Arkansas.

Three more days of driving made me even grumpier.

Between Dad playing screaming old rock-and-roll music for hours on end and roughly three thousand games of tic-tac-toe with Harper and so many peanut butter and jelly sandwiches that I felt like I might

die if I ever saw another one, I hated just about everyone and everything.

Maybe I liked seeing the world's largest bottle of
hair tonic in Oklahoma and standing in New Mexico,
Utah, Arizona, and Colorado all at the same time—
but I'd never *admit* it.

And anyway, none of that mattered, now that we
were almost to our new home.

Nevada was ugly. Okay, so the mountains were
nice. But there wasn't anything on them. No trees.
Nothing green. We were moving to a very brown
state.

It didn't have the Atlantic Ocean. No boardwalk.
Probably no hoagies. Definitely no Wildwood Middle
School. I hated Nevada and no one could convince
me otherwise.

I was still in the car, grinding my teeth, waiting
as long as I dared before I got out to help unpack the
trailer, when I saw her.

She was about my age, twelve-ish, with dark hair
hanging in two braids almost to her waist, and she
was tall and skinny. Grandma Ellen would have said

that she was all knees and elbows. And she would have been right.

What yanked me right out of my sourness, though, was everything else about her.

She wore cutoff jeans and a white T-shirt with purple polka dots. Pretty standard stuff. But she also had rainbow-striped socks pulled up to her bony knees and roller skates that looked like blue-and-yellow running shoes strapped to her feet. And over her clothes, she wore a red swimsuit with a purple stripe running down each side. She had something tied around her neck, flapping in the hot, dry breeze as she skated in slow circles on her porch.

Was this strange girl my new next-door neighbor? She looked like she came from another planet. Despite myself, I was curious enough to open the car door and step my first foot in Nev-a-da.

I felt a little bit like Han Solo or Indiana Jones. An explorer, exploring new lands with strange creatures. And that was kind of cool.

"See, there's a kid next door," Dad said, rubbing my head as he passed me. "You're going to be fine, Boss."

I ducked away from his hand and looked at the girl to check if she was watching. She wasn't. Her eyes stayed on the road that ran in front of our houses.

I looked that way, too. She seemed to be waiting for someone, but not even a single car had driven by since we pulled into our new driveway.

Our street was just her house and ours, next to each other with one other house on either side. Just four houses with a wide patch of bare desert across the street, and some kind of farm behind.

Whoever she was, she was focused on the empty street. She didn't even seem to notice me.

I mean, us.

Step #1: ignore her back.

I walked back and forth with boxes of dishes and books and clothes. I stacked two boxes on top of each other. I tried for three the next trip, but Mom stopped me before I could break something.

The girl didn't even glance my way.

Step #2: boss Harper.

I marched my little sister around the yard like a drill sergeant.

"Hurry up," I told her. "And don't forget, that box goes in the bathroom."

"I don't have to do what you tell me to, Giddy," she said. "Mom said so."

Harper was five and young enough to still get away with all kinds of stuff I'd never slip past our parents. Case in point: she stuck out her tongue, even though Mom was right there. Then she headed off to unpack her dolls when I tried to make her carry my skateboard into the garage.

The girl next door still didn't look at me.

I mean, us.

I didn't have a step #3.

When the trailer was finally empty, I was sent to my new room to make up my bed and start to unpack. Instead, I stood at my window and watched her skate in her slow circles between her front door and the edge of the porch steps. She never took her eyes off the road. Never once looked up at me.

Two

New Jersey summers are sticky, humid scorchers, but Nevada was something else altogether. We'd moved into a blast furnace. Outside my bedroom window the sky was a clear, cloudless blue. It looked like a nice day, until you opened a door and ran into a wall of heat.

When the doorbell rang the next morning, I was lying on my bed with a fan blowing on my face, and my well-worn copy of *The Hobbit* on my chest ready to grab if Mom came in to check up on me.

Lying around was not an approved activity in the Quinton household.

I grabbed the book and fumbled it open when Mom called out, "Gideon! Gideon, come here."

Was she seriously going to make me meet some

neighborhood lady who'd come to snoop out what kind of crazy family would move to this hot, dry, dusty place?

In a small show of rebellion, I went out into the living room in just my dinosaur pajama bottoms. I rounded the corner and then came to a dead stop.

Why hadn't I put on a pair of jeans?

And a shirt.

I would have given anything for a T-shirt right then. The girl who had completely ignored me the day before watched me with careful eyes so dark brown, they were nearly black. Her hair floated around her in a wild cloud of brown curls.

Mom's back was to me, her neat blond hair in stark contrast, and she was asking the girl about the middle school.

"Gideon will be in the seventh grade."

"Me, too," the girl said.

"Do you like your teachers?"

She shook her head. "Not really."

"Oh. I . . . really?" Impressive. Mom wasn't caught off guard very often. Like, never.

I took a step backward, but Mom turned and saw

me. Her eyes dropped down to my pajama pants and she gave me a look that said, plain as day, *natural consequences, Gideon.*

In other words—this is what I get for lying around in my pj's all morning.

"Gideon, this is Roona. She lives next door."

The night before, all I wanted was for Roona to notice me. I didn't even know why it was so important. Now she pushed her hair off her forehead and stared at me, and I wished I could sink into the floor. I finally managed to get out, "Hi."

"Hi," Roona said. "Want to go swimming?"

My eyebrows shot up. "You have a pool?"

"Sure. Everyone in Logandale has a pool. Haven't you felt how hot it is here?"

"I want to go swimming." Harper bounced on her toes. The end of her blond ponytail twitched like a cat's tail.

"No way," I said.

"Mom!"

"That's enough, Harper." Mom tilted her head and gave the exact answer I knew was coming. "I don't know. Is your mother home, Roona?"

"Yes, ma'am," Roona said, sweet as pie.

I felt the *maybe another day* coming before Mom opened her mouth, and my disappointment was sudden and sharp. I scrambled for an alternative that might keep Roona at our house. A game of Monopoly? Riding bikes?

Mom surprised me, though. "Go ahead, get changed, Gideon."

"Me, too?" Harper asked, already headed for her new bedroom to find her swimsuit.

"Not this time, Sweetpea."

Harper pouted and I blinked. I needed a second to absorb this turn of events. "Okay," I said slowly, expecting the other shoe to drop.

"I'll walk over with you and meet Mrs. . . ."

"Mulroney," Roona said.

There it was. Not too bad, though. I ran into my room, traded my dinosaur pajamas for a pair of swim trunks that I had to dig through three boxes to find, then ran back before Mom could change her mind.

*M*y mom and Roona's didn't look like they came from the same planet. Mine wore a white dress that covered her knees and her arms to her elbows, even though it was about a thousand degrees outside, sandals, and lipstick. Roona's wore denim overalls, was in her bare feet, and was covered with flour.

I couldn't remember the last time I'd seen my mom walk around in her bare feet.

Mrs. Mulroney paid attention to me before she even looked at my mom. She smiled and said, "You're the boy who moved in yesterday. I told Roona I thought you were just her age. Seventh grade?"

"Oh. Yeah. When school starts again."

"Daria Quinton," Mom said, holding out her hand between me and Mrs. Mulroney like she was at a business meeting or something. Mom had never been to a business meeting, as far as I knew, so I wasn't sure what she was doing.

Mrs. Mulroney wiped her hands on the back of her overalls, then shook with Mom. "Miranda Mulroney."

They held hands for maybe a second too long. Mom took hers back first. "Roona invited Gideon for a swim, but if you're busy—it looks like you're cooking."

"No, it's fine," Mrs. Mulroney said. "I was going to come say hello today. I had to get an early start on these scones."

"Scones?"

Mrs. Mulroney smiled. She was probably the prettiest woman I'd ever seen up close, and I wondered if that was why Mom was acting so weird. Girls were weird in general, so I wasn't sure.

"For the chamber of commerce breakfast tomorrow morning," Mrs. Mulroney said.

"My mom bakes for all of the events around here," Roona said.

Mrs. Mulroney smiled and put a hand on the back of Roona's head, smoothing the wild curls. "I just picked up raspberries fresh at the farmers' market. Would you like a scone?"

"No, thank you." Mom didn't eat gluten anymore. Gluten is basically in everything that's baked and tastes good. She tried to make us all stop, but that didn't last long thanks to Dad. "Another day might be better for that swim."

"Please, Mom," I said, but low, under my breath.

She looked down at me, then said, "If you're sure he won't be in your way."

"Oh, I'm sure. He'll keep Roona occupied so I can get this last batch in the oven."

Roona's swimming pool was plastic, eight inches deep, and filled with a garden hose. I stared at it, caught between disappointment and not wanting to *show* my disappointment. At least it was in the shade of the house. Otherwise, I think I might have melted. The water inside it was as warm as a bath.

We sat in folding chairs that scorched the backs of our thighs; our feet dangled in the shallow water. We'd already covered the basics. Roona was an only child who had lived in Logandale all her life. Her dad was in the air force and her mom was a baker. I missed New Jersey and had a little sister named Harper. My dad was an artist, but he worked in marketing. My mom was a nurse and worked in an emergency room before I was born, but now she was just a mom.

Silence stretched between us as we kicked at the water with bare toes. It didn't do anything to cool us off. The awkwardness got to me, and as happy as I was to have someone to hang out with, I wondered if it was lunchtime yet.

Roona said, "Let's play Truth."

"Truth?"

"Like Truth or Dare—only just truths. Two rules. We have to answer and we have to tell the truth."

My stomach tightened. I'd never liked new things and it seemed like this new thing could go particularly bad. "I think I have to go check in."

"No you don't," she said. "It's only ten thirty."

Shoot.

"Well—what kind of questions?"

"Whatever kind we want. It's our game."

"What if one of us really, really doesn't want to answer?"

Roona wrinkled her nose and thought for a minute, then said, "Okay, we each get one pass."

This is what my dad would call being caught between a rock and a hard place. Roona was the closest thing I had to a potential friend so far in Nevada. I hadn't even seen any other kids in our new neighborhood. If I blew her off, it was going to be a long, lonely summer—and I'd have to start seventh grade without any friends at all.

"Do any other kids live on our street?" I asked.

"Is that really the first question you want to ask?"

"What? No. I was just curious."

"This whole game is about being curious." Roona straightened her pigtails over her shoulders and said, "No other kids. Ready to start?"

Not even close, but even though I'd already had the thought myself, I didn't want *her* to decide it was time for me to go check in with my mom, so I said, "Fine."

She clapped her hands and sat up straighter in her chair. "You go first."

"Wait." My brain seized up, like it had never heard of a question before. "What?"

"Ask me something. Anything. It doesn't matter what it is."

"Um . . ." *Don't say something stupid. Don't say something stupid.* "What's your favorite color?"

She quirked an eyebrow in a perfect arch. Man, I wished I could do that. "Yellow."

"Mine's blue," I said.

"I didn't ask, so that doesn't count."

"Okay."

"Wait. Should we both answer all the questions?" she asked, very seriously.

"Sure," I said. "I mean, I guess so."

"Favorite movie."

Umm. Umm. The only thing I could think of was the movie Harper watched about three thousand times on Dad's iPad during the drive from New Jersey. It came blurting out before I could stop it. *"Finding Nemo."*

"Beauty and the Beast."

Okay. Okay. "Favorite song."

"Anything by the Beatles."

My brain went blank again. Her answer was too *cool.* Why couldn't she have said some boy band? It felt like someone had filled my empty skull with concrete. "Uh . . ."

"Just say the first song you think of."

The only song I could put my finger on was my mom's favorite song. "'With or Without You.' You know, U2?"

She nodded with appreciation and I warmed up

to the game. She asked, "Last time you brushed your teeth."

I'd forgotten before I went to bed the night before and I almost lied, but for some reason I just couldn't. "Yesterday morning."

"This morning."

Middle names. Douglas and Louise.

Favorite soda. We both liked Dr Pepper.

Favorite ice cream. I liked chocolate. She liked rainbow sherbet.

Favorite holiday. I liked Christmas. She liked Arbor Day.

"Arbor Day?"

"I like trees," she said. "Do you like to read?"

"Yes."

"Me, too."

"Favorite book?"

"The Hobbit."

I blinked. "Really?"

"Yes," she said, a little defensive.

"Me, too."

She looked at me different, like that answer meant something more than I was a nerd who liked old books that none of my friends had ever read. Then she nodded like she'd come to some kind of decision and said, "What's the scariest thing that's ever happened to you?"

That question was quite a lot deeper than the others and I felt myself closing up. I wished I was back home—not next door in a house that didn't feel like mine, but back home in New Jersey. "I don't know."

"Yes you do," she said.

I did. I could have stood up, shoved my wet feet into my flip-flops, and left, but something kept me there—as if the plastic chair had melted to my butt and glued me to it. "You go first."

Roona's mouth tightened into a flat line as she considered the proposed break in the rules. Finally she said, "My mom almost died when I was in the third grade."

I opened my mouth, but nothing came out. I was expecting a story about someone jumping out at her on Halloween or maybe something closer to my own scariest story. I had never even really thought about one of my parents dying. Never once in my whole life. I finally managed to ask, "How?"

"She took too much medicine."

This was the very definition of Too Much Information, and I wasn't sure what to say. I had a vague idea that taking too much medicine was something that might be an accident, but might not be, too. I couldn't ask about that. It was too personal. "What did you do?"

"I had to go live with my aunt Jane for the rest of the school year." Roona leaned down and scooped a fly out of the pool, flinging it into the yard. "My aunt Jane has eight kids. Gertie, Amaleah, Tucker, Lola, Everett and Morgan, Harvest, and baby Joe. They ran out of names, I think."

"Oh." I squirmed and tried to come up with something neutral to ask. "Where do they live?"

"On a farm in Boise with chickens and goats and a pig named Bruiser. He pulls the kids around in a cart."

"The pig does?"

"Yes." Roona shifted in her chair. She looked uncomfortable, like there was something more she wanted to say, but she just sat back. "Your turn."

I was so taken aback by her story that mine just came blurting out. "I got lost once."

"Where?"

She wasn't supposed to ask another question. That wasn't part of the game, but I answered anyway because I'd asked extra questions, too. "At a gas station."

"How old were you?"

"Four," I said. She didn't ask another question. She didn't say anything at all, which had the same effect. I kept talking to fill the silence. "I didn't really get lost."

"You were left?" she asked quietly.

I'd never told anyone, not even my dad. I'd never talked about it with my mom. She probably thought I didn't remember. It took years for me to get old enough to understand what had happened that day.

You aren't supposed to remember much about being four years old, but I remembered. I didn't get lost. She forgot me. We stopped for gas halfway to Grandma Ellen's house in Philadelphia and she let me out to stretch my legs. After she filled the tank, she got back in the car and drove away while I stood on the curb between the pumps.

"Did she come right back?" Roona asked.

I shook my head. I'd only heard her talk about it once. When I was in the second grade she told a friend that she didn't remember me until she'd hugged her mother, who asked *where's my baby boy?* It gave me a weird, sick feeling in my gut.

"Someone called the police. They fed me a Happy Meal while they tried to find someone who knew me." I swallowed. "Your turn."

Roona inhaled, then exhaled slowly. "Did you see my blanket last night?"

"Tied around your neck?"

"Yes."

"It was hard to miss."

"It saved my life when I was a baby. I was bundled in it like a burrito when our house caught fire. My dad busted in and picked me up, right out of the flames."

She had a way of telling a story that felt equal parts absolutely true and totally made-up.

"I would have burned up or smoked like a

sausage," she told me. "I would have, but my blanket saved me long enough for my dad to get me. Sometimes I think I can still smell smoke on it."

I didn't know what to say, so I stayed quiet and she kept talking.

Her father joined the air force soon after and she'd never seen him again. She didn't remember any of it. Not the fire. Not her father saving her. She had no memories of her father at all.

"Don't they let soldiers come home sometimes?" I asked.

Roona shrugged and I wished I'd kept my question to myself. "I think he must have a super-important job. He's going to come home soon, though. I know it."

I bit my bottom lip, holding back my next question. But then I had to know. "Were you waiting for him last night? When you were skating on your porch?"

She was. Her mother had told her the story of her father's bravery and how the blanket had protected her. She wrapped Roona in the blanket every night for years. Told her that it made her Wonder Roo and gave her superpowers. It didn't fit around her anymore, so now she wore it like a cape.

"It's still got power," she said. "It still makes me Wonder Roo."

Tooth Fairy magic, I thought. Santa Claus magic. Hobbit magic. The kind of magic that I maybe believed in, but probably not. But I didn't say so. The truth was, I wasn't quite sure.

She'd told two scary stories, one about each of her parents, and I was desperate to balance things out with another story of my own. But I had nothing exciting or scary or adventurous that had happened to me since I was four years old.

I was a Quinton, through and through. I'd never wanted more excitement or scariness or adventure in my life. But I wanted to believe in Wonder Roo, the same way I wanted to believe in Middle-earth. So I came up with one more story.

"My grandma Ellen is magic," I blurted out.

Roona's eyebrows shot up. "What?"

"She is." I felt my sudden burst of bravery popping

like a soap bubble. Oh God. This was a bad idea. "She is magic."

"What kind of magic?" Roona asked.

I'd started down this path and I kept moving down it, like I wasn't in charge of the words coming out of my mouth. "She can pull quarters out of my ears."

Roona stared at me for what felt like an hour, but was probably five seconds. Long enough for me to think: she's going to laugh at me, and this is going to be the most horrible, boring summer of all time.

Then Roona did laugh. But it was an eye-crinkling, bent-at-the-waist kind of laughter that made me think I'd do almost anything to hear it again.

Three

*B*efore we moved, my parents argued (a lot) about whether or not to let me finish my school year in Wildwood. Mom was worried that I'd spend the whole summer moping around with no friends if I didn't finish the school year in Nevada. Dad was worried that being the new kid at the end of the school year would scar me for life.

In a rare turn of events, Dad won. It was what I wanted, but now I was in the desert facing a long, hot, dry summer with no friends except the curious girl who lived next door, who may or may not have superpowers.

To say I was intrigued would be putting it mildly. Without much of anything else to occupy my mind, I couldn't stop thinking about Roona.

That afternoon, I watched out my bedroom window while Roona skated in circles on her front porch, watching the street. I wanted to talk to her some more, but she never looked up at my window. I was way too shy to leave my own hobbit-hole and go to her house, uninvited.

The next morning, I got my wish. Roona crossed back over into my home territory. She banged on our front door and when I answered it, she said, all breathless, "Want to go to the movies?"

I looked over my shoulder, but Mom didn't come out of the kitchen.

"My mom's taking us." Roona's face was lit up like a Christmas tree. She grabbed my hand. "You don't want to miss this."

I looked down at her fingers tight around my palm and suddenly, I really didn't want to miss it. *I'm going on an adventure.* "I'll ask."

I left her at the door and went to the kitchen. Mom was making gluten-free banana bread—her glass-half-full response to learning that bananas lasted approximately a day and a half in the Nevada heat.

"Mom." When she didn't answer right away, I said, "Mom. Mom."

"Gideon," she said. "Gideon. Gideon."

"Can I go to the movies with Roona and her mom?"

Mom wiped her hands on a towel. "I don't know, honey. We still have a lot of unpacking to do."

"It's just a movie. I promise I'll help when I get home. Please?"

The fact that since the last time I was with Roona I'd spent my time committing that cardinal Quinton-family sin—absolutely nothing—probably played in my favor. Mom looked through the kitchen into the living room at Roona bouncing on her toes, bursting with excitement to hang out with me, and said, "Well, okay. Take ten dollars out of my wallet. Don't buy candy."

I did try to do as I was told.

I bought buttered popcorn and a Slurpee suicide. That's a little of each flavor. It was pure sugar, but not technically candy. Mom wouldn't have allowed it. Not in a million years.

It was Mrs. Mulroney who pulled a handful of Pixy Stix from her purse. Roona kept half and gave me the other half. I didn't *buy* the candy. Mom didn't say anything about eating it. "Thanks."

"Have you seen this one?" Mrs. Mulroney asked, leaning over Roona.

I snapped one of the Pixy Stix with a flick of my wrist, to send the sugar to one end, as I shook my head. We were sitting in the very, very front row, even though most of the seats were empty. I had never sat in the front of a theater before. I had to tilt my head back to see the whole screen. "We've been busy, you know, moving and all."

Mrs. Mulroney sat back as the lights dimmed. I opened the paper tube and poured a pile of sour sweetness onto my tongue.

"We've seen it six times," Roona whispered.

I swallowed and coughed a little when the powdery candy went down funny. "What?"

She shushed me, waving a hand as the first previews started.

There had been no discussion about which movie we'd see. Mrs. Mulroney didn't even ask for my ten-dollar bill. She just bought three tickets to a cartoon about forest animals who try to rescue their friend who winds up in the suburbs. Who sees a movie like that six times in the theater?

It took about fifteen minutes, and two more Pixy Stix, for it to become very clear that Mrs. Mulroney really had seen this film six times. And she liked it. A *lot*.

She started to sing. Not under her breath, either. She sang loud and clear, as if she really was a girl raccoon who was about to accidentally hitch a ride in a picnic basket.

I slunk down in my seat, cheeks burning. It wasn't that she sang poorly. In fact, she had a nice voice. But I thought about my own mother doing anything at all, especially in public, with so much gusto, and so *loud*, and I wanted to crawl under my seat.

I was embarrassed for Roona, but she wasn't embarrassed at all. She smiled up at her mother, then started to sing, too.

Mrs. Mulroney stood up as the song built to its

high point. The audience behind us started to hiss at her. She shook her hips and raised her arms over her head, singing the girl raccoon's song at the top of her lungs. She grabbed Roona and pulled her to her feet. Roona reached back and grabbed my hand.

I tried to pull it back. "I can't."

"Come on, Gideon," Roona said, stretched between her mother and me, already starting to dance. "YOLO!"

"What?"

"You only live once."

If I didn't get up, she'd let go of me. She'd dance in front of the movie screen with her mother and neither of them would care whether or not I joined them. Someone yelled *sit down!* and I came to my feet with my heart in my stomach. I wanted to be part of their fun, even though the idea of it scared me more than anything I'd ever done before.

Roona's face lit up and she started to sing with her mother again.

Oh God. Oh God. I shifted my weight from one foot to the other, the best I could manage as far as dancing was concerned. The first line I tried to sing caught in my throat.

Then something Tookish woke up in me and overcame my natural Quinton reserve. My bones let loose and my throat did, too. The second line came out more easily as I found my groove.

Management came down the aisle before the song was over. Mrs. Mulroney squealed and picked up her purse. She grabbed Roona by the hand. Roona grabbed me, and we cracked the whip toward the exit at the front of the theater. Mrs. Mulroney pressed her weight into the bar and the door opened, triggering an alarm that caused the whole audience to cry out.

We ran like lunatics to the parking lot.

"Now what?" Mrs. Mulroney asked when we were in her little yellow VW bug, red-faced and hiccuping with laughter. I was caught somewhere between mildly in love with both of them and half-dead with shock at my own nerve. "I can't believe that just happened."

"Fro-yo!!" Roona said.

"Fro-yo," Mrs. Mulroney agreed.

I collapsed back in my seat. I'd just experienced more excitement than I had in my entire life. The Quintons did not sing and dance at movies. We didn't even sing and dance in our own living room. And we certainly did not get chased out of theaters or set off alarms. We did not eat Pixy Stix and frozen yogurt in the same day.

We were more of a sit-quietly-in-the-back, watch-singing-and-dancing-on-TV-without-leaving-the-sofa, whole-wheat-spaghetti kind of family. Or we were, until Mom stopped eating gluten. Now we were a quinoa-and-broccoli kind of family.

Mrs. Mulroney drove us to a frozen yogurt place. The kind where you can add your own toppings. They piled marshmallows, teddy bear graham crackers, and chocolate chips in their bowls. Guilt caught up with me and I went for strawberries and walnuts.

The two of them sang the songs from the movie while we ate. I didn't know any of them, so I was just on the outside looking in, basking in the strange energy that radiated from Mrs. Mulroney and seemed to infect Roona.

Between the Slurpee, the candy, and the frozen yogurt, plus the adrenaline rush, I was feeling a little woozy by the time we pulled into their driveway an hour later. I wasn't worried about Mom finding out what I'd been up to. She'd never believe it, even if I told her.

"I have to make a blueberry pie tonight," Mrs. Mulroney announced after she cut the engine.

For some reason, the energy of the day plummeted. Roona sat up straighter and shook her head. Mrs. Mulroney sighed and it was as if all of her laughter and raccoon songs blew out with her breath.

"Not tonight," Roona said. "Tomorrow."

"Miss Oberman is expecting it, first thing in the morning." Mrs. Mulroney opened the car door. "For her mother's birthday."

Roona sat back while her mother got out and walked toward the house. "This is bad."

I leaned forward, between the front seats. "What do you mean?"

"Blueberry is always bad."

"Why?"

She didn't answer.

"*Y*ou went on a date with Roona," Harper said.

"No I didn't."

She wheeled her scooter around me in a circle as I tried to walk toward our house. "Oh yes, you did."

"Shut up, Harper." I brushed past her and walked faster.

"Giddy and Roona sitting in a tree . . . K-I-S-S-I-N-G . . ."

"You are so *stupid*!" I went inside and slammed the door.

Mom and Dad were unpacking books in the living room and they both stopped and looked up at me.

"Hey," Dad said. "What did that door do to you?"

I shook my head. "Why can't I be an only child?"

He thought for a moment, then said, "We knew you were going to need to learn patience and resilience. Really, we did you a favor."

"Resilience?" I asked.

I should have known better. Mom picked a

book off the shelf she was filling and handed it to me.

A dictionary.

Ugh. "I'll just Google it."

"How was the movie?" she asked.

I didn't know how to begin to tell her the truth, so I just said, "It was okay."

Four

The next morning Roona bypassed our front door altogether and knocked on my bedroom window. I opened my curtains, rubbing sleep from my eyes.

"What are you doing here?"

"Miss Oberman already picked it up," Roona said.

"What?"

"The blueberry pie. We have to stop her before she delivers it."

"Why?"

"Just come over, okay?" She looked down at my dinosaur pajamas. "Get dressed first."

Mom wouldn't let me leave our house without eating breakfast and she wouldn't let me go to anyone else's house, not even our next-door neighbor's, before eight a.m.

After I ate some banana bread, I sat at the kitchen table fully dressed, with my shoes on, watching the clock tick slowly, slowly from 7:34 to 8:00.

The instant it did, I went into my parents' bedroom. It was Friday and Dad didn't start his new job until Monday. He was going to work in marketing at a casino on the outskirts of the most outskirt town in the world. So they were both in there. They'd made a little two-person chain: Mom pulled clothes out of a box and put them on hangers. Dad hung them in the closet.

"Can I go to Roona's?"

"Your room," Mom said.

"I promise to finish it after lunch." I looked at Dad. "Please?"

He said, "I have to go in to sign some papers at human resources this afternoon. Your whole room unpacked by the time I get home sounds great to me."

"I don't know about my *whole* room," I said.

He held out his hands, like it wasn't up to him, then pointed his forefingers at me. "It was your plan,

Boss. Have fun with Roona this morning, then get to work."

Mom lifted her eyebrows and I said, "Okay, fine."

"Can I go?" Harper asked from the bedroom door. "I want to go."

"No way."

"Mommm! I want to go with Gideon."

"I need your help here, Harper."

Harper pouted and I left while I had the chance.

*R*oona answered her door and said, "Took you long enough."

"I had to wait until eight. What's the big deal anyway?"

"We have to get that pie back."

"But *why*?"

"I really hope it's not too late already." She led me to her bedroom. It was a shocking mess. Piles of books, half-drawn pictures, what looked like every toy she'd ever owned from the time she was a baby. Clothes everywhere.

"Roona, why do we have to get the pie back?"

She got on her hands and knees and lifted her

bed skirt, shoved her head underneath it, and rooted around. "Just trust me."

"I trust you," I said. "But I still want to know."

Roona gave a little whoop and sat up, holding an orange swimsuit with a green flower. "Found it! Operation Blueberry Pie is a go."

"Roona."

Her legs were so long and skinny, she reminded me of a camel as she got back to her feet. Roona shoved one leg and then the other into the swimsuit and pulled the stretchy fabric right up over her cutoff jeans and T-shirt.

"What are you doing?" I asked.

"This is going to take Wonder Roo."

I laughed, but she didn't laugh with me, so I stopped. "Operation Blueberry Pie?"

"That's right."

"Why is it going to take Wonder Roo?"

"Because blueberries are blue."

"I know," I said. "It's right there in the name."

"Blue is a *sad* color." I waited for her to go on. Roona sighed and sat on the edge of her bed. "Mom baked Miss Oberman's pie in the middle of the night, when she thought I was asleep. She only does that when she doesn't want me to know how sad she is."

"You weren't asleep?"

"How could I sleep when the whole house was filling up with tears?"

"What?"

"They got into the pie, Gideon."

"The tears?"

"Of course."

I watched her pull up her rainbow socks from her long toes to her scabbed knees. "I don't get it."

She put her feet on the ground and looked at me. "Tears in a blueberry pie are extra bad."

I leaned forward, caught up in her words. "How?"

She pulled her feet up and crossed them under her, settling in. "Last year Mom baked a cake for Fletcher Dorrance's sixth birthday. Do you know him?"

"No," I said.

"No. You don't. How could you?" Roona looked out her bedroom window at the patch of desert across the street. "Fletcher's mother hired my mom to bake a birthday cake, with fish and boats and a whale on top. It was the most beautiful cake she'd ever made."

"That doesn't sound so bad," I said.

"Mom was sad the day she decorated Fletcher Dorrance's birthday cake. So sad that she filled our house with her tears. Just like *Alice in Wonderland*. They splashed around her knees while she baked. They ruined my backpack. The cat floated into the laundry room."

I couldn't bring myself to call her a liar, but it was close. "Not really, though."

"It's true. She missed my dad" was all that Roona said about why her mother cried so much. "She always misses my dad, but some days she misses him harder than others. Her tears had mixed into the blue cake batter."

"Gross."

"It was a fantastic cake. There was a pirate ship made entirely of chocolate," Roona said. "And a school of dolphins jumping from the waves around the edges. The whale was a work of art. Fletcher's mother said she hated to cut into it."

I sat on the floor at her feet and leaned into Roona's story. "What happened?"

"First Fletcher's little sister, Amanda, started to cry."

I leaned back a little. "Little sisters always cry. Harper cries all the time."

She held up one finger, then added a second to it. "Xavier Harris started to cry."

"Oh." But still. Two kids crying at a six-year-old's birthday party?

"Then Lilliana. Then Mariana. Then Kariana. All the Anas started crying, one after the other." The rest of her fingers popped up.

"All of them?" I asked.

"Every one of them." She held up her other hand. "Then Marcus and his brother, Lucas, who was there to keep Amanda company. And Hillary and Margot. And by that time, Fletcher was so upset that everyone else was crying and getting all the attention on his birthday that he started to cry, too."

"Wow."

"So now Mrs. Dorrance is so flustered trying to make every six-year-old in the neighborhood stop crying that *she* starts crying. And Mr. Dorrance, who has no patience for crying—everyone knows that—storms in to find out what all the fuss was about." Roona sat back and crossed her arms over her chest. "And he nearly drowned in all the tears."

I blinked. "That's not true."

"Yes it is. They up and moved to Cleveland," Roona said, "the very next week."

I sat up, released from her spell. "That's not true, though."

"Of course it is."

"No one can cry enough to fill up a house with tears."

Her face clouded. "Yes they can."

My mouth opened to argue, but I closed it again. I couldn't help it. I believed her. Or at least I didn't *not* believe her. "Who is Miss Oberman anyway?"

"She was my mom's teacher in the second grade," Roona said. "Mine, too. She must be a hundred and ten years old."

"No one is a hundred and ten years old," I pointed out. "Why does Miss Oberman need a blueberry pie?"

"She's taking it to her mother, down to the old folks' home."

"Is her mother a hundred and fifty?" I asked.

"At least." Roona unfolded her legs and reached for her roller skates. "We have to hurry. You can bring your bike and I'll hitch a ride on the back."

"Uhh," I said. "Where's the old folks' home?"

Roona wrinkled her nose, thinking. "About a mile away."

I shook my head. "I'm not allowed to ride my bike that far. I'm not even allowed to cross the street."

"Are you serious?" Roona looked at me like she'd never heard of a kid with boundaries before. I felt my face burn. "You are. You're not allowed to cross the street?"

"Well, I wasn't in New Jersey. It wasn't like here." I swept my arm toward the desert outside her window. "There were way more people and much more traffic."

"Okay. Are you coming or not? I have to get that pie."

"Um . . ."

She smiled at me and went to her bedroom door. "It's okay. I'll just see you later."

She went out without even looking back at me, to make sure I left with her.

"Wait," I said, before I could stop myself. Forget butterflies. I had bats in my stomach, turning somersaults. "I'll go."

*R*oona held on to the rack on the back of my bike and crouched low, the wheels of her roller skates whizzing along the blacktop, while I pedaled so hard and fast, I thought we might take off in flight at any moment.

I was terrified that she'd hit a rock and send us both crashing into the blacktop, but she didn't seem worried at all. She had her blanket around her neck and when I looked over my shoulder, I saw it flapping behind her like a real superhero cape.

The old folks' home was more like two miles away, I guessed. Much farther than my mother, who was used to giving me city boundaries, would have allowed me to go if I'd bothered to ask.

She would have told me not to cross any streets, limiting my world to just our block. But this was a state of emergency, or at least Roona was sure it was. That meant saying sorry if we were caught, instead of asking permission ahead of time.

Bilbo Baggins from *The Hobbit* would agree. He would have gone on this Operation Blueberry Pie adventure, too. The blanket cracked in the wind as I tried to go a little faster.

The old folks' home wasn't really a home. It looked like a school to me. A long, low building with a parking lot in front and an office smack in the middle.

Roona pointed to an old pickup truck in a handicapped spot near the front and said, "Miss Oberman's already here."

She sat on the curb and took off her skates, tied their laces together, flung them over one shoulder, and walked in her striped socks to the front door. I followed, mostly because after coming this far there was no way I was missing whatever was next.

The front door had a little keypad lock. Roona pressed her freckled face to the glass, one hand on either side, and peered in.

"Oh no," she said, low, under her breath. "Oh no."

"What? What is it?"

I stood beside her and looked through the dark glass, too.

All I saw was a nurse standing beside a frail old man, her arm around him, their heads pressed close together.

"It's started already," Roona said. "We're too late."

"How do you know?"

"Can't you see? They're crying."

"Are you sure? They look like they're talking."

Roona shook her head and pulled her cape from around her neck. She folded it neatly and stuck it under her arm. "No way."

"'Scuse me," someone said, and we both jumped.

A man stood behind us. He kept his eyes on Roona, and I didn't blame him. She looked ridiculous with her swimsuit worn over her clothes and those silly socks.

He reached past me to punch some numbers into the keypad. Roona grabbed the door before it closed all the way and we walked into the old folks' home.

It smelled like the stuff Grandma Ellen used to clean her toilets and those mushy frozen peas, and under all of it, like Harper's room when she still wore diapers.

The floors were covered in white tiles and the walls were painted a slightly bluer white. The bright lights overhead made the whole place feel cold and harsh. Roona was right. The nurse and the old man were both crying.

Roona walked right up to the high counter. The woman behind it didn't notice us. She was crying, too, quietly, into a wad of tissues. I looked at my feet. So far the old folks' home wasn't filling up with tears, but I couldn't deny it. The crying *was* an awful coincidence.

"Pardon me," Roona said.

The woman finally looked at us. Then she glanced around, probably for a grown-up. "Roona? What are you doing here?"

Roona said, "We need to see Miss Oberman."

"Miss Oberman?" The woman was distracted by the old man and his nurse. She blew her nose into her tissues.

"Yes, ma'am."

"Well, you can't go back to the resident rooms without a parent, honey. Is Miranda here?"

"But we have to," Roona said. "It's life or death."

That got the lady's attention. "What do you mean, life or death?"

Roona took a small step back. Inspiration struck and before I could think better of it, I made her my great-grandma and said, "She's my nana."

"Mrs. Oberman is?" the woman asked.

"Yes, ma'am. Someone's already inside waiting for us."

"Who?"

I almost said *my grandma*, but Roona kept calling Mrs. Oberman's daughter *Miss* Oberman and I wasn't sure if she had kids. The receptionist would probably know. She knew Roona, after all. "My aunt is already inside. My, um, great-aunt Oberman."

A big black book sat on the counter. The woman pulled it down to her desk and looked at it. "Why didn't you come in with her?"

"My mom just dropped us off." I wondered if lying to the receptionist at an old folks' home was a felony or a misdemeanor. Roona Louise Mulroney was definitely a bad influence.

Roona's dark eyes darted to me and I had to look away or I was going to do or say something to give away my lie.

"Okay." The woman wiped tears from her face with the back of her hand, then dried them with the same tissues she'd blown her nose into. "Next time, your mom needs to come in with you. Sign here and you can go see your nana."

She put the book back and turned it toward us. Roona scribbled her name, then gave me the pen and I did the same, even though I had a twinge of doubt about leaving a paper trail. Just above Roona's name was Miss Oberman—the daughter—signed in to see Mrs. Oberman—the mother—in room 115.

As we followed signs toward the right hallway, we saw two more crying nurses and three crying old folks.

"She couldn't have given them all pie," I said.

I was still pretty sure that a blueberry pie couldn't make people cry so much that they flooded an old folks' home—but panic built a small fire under my ribs.

Room 99.

Room 101.

Room 103. Two women sat on the edge of one bed, both sobbing.

Room 105.

Room 107.

Room 109. The door was closed, but we heard the wails and started to walk faster.

Room 111.

Room 113.

Finally, room 115. The door was closed and I stopped walking, but Roona opened it and went right in. I followed, because the other option was staying alone in the cold, smelly hallway that might very well flood with tears at any moment.

Inside, a very old woman stood near the window with tears streaming down her face. I would have thought she was the oldest woman I'd ever seen, with her perfectly white hair and soft, wrinkled skin, only the woman in the wheelchair beside her was even older. She was crying, too.

"Roona?" the younger old woman said. "Roona Mulroney, what are you doing here?"

"You already gave them the pie, didn't you?"

Roona said. Then she looked at the even older woman. "Happy birthday, Mrs. Oberman."

"Thank you, darling."

Miss Oberman's bottom lip trembled. "We were eating it when we heard the news."

"What news?" I asked, then winced when both old ladies looked at me. "Sorry."

"Mrs. Franklin died this morning." Miss Oberman sat on the edge of her mother's bed. "It's the saddest story I've ever heard."

"And the sweetest," her mother said.

"Yes. And the sweetest."

Roona put her roller skates on the floor. "Who is Mrs. Franklin?"

"A lovely, lovely woman. She moved here with her husband a few months ago. Mr. Franklin wasn't expected to live long and she couldn't stand to let him come alone."

"But he got better," the elder Mrs. Oberman said. "He's healthy as a horse now."

"It's remarkable that she should go first." The younger Miss Oberman blew her nose with a mighty honk. "Just remarkable. And now he's just lost."

Roona looked at me and I tried to tell her with my eyes that a blueberry pie didn't have anything to do with Mr. and Mrs. Franklin, even if her mother had been crying when she made it.

"Is there pie left?" Roona asked.

Miss Oberman shook her head. "It was a nice breakfast surprise, though, wasn't it, Mother?"

"Yes," Mrs. Oberman said. "Yes it was. Tell Miranda thank you for me, won't you?"

"Yes, ma'am." Roona picked up her skates. "I'm sorry I didn't get here in time."

"In time for pie? I'm sure your mother will bake you another one if you ask." Roona looked horrified, but Miss Oberman didn't seem to notice. She was looking at me. "Who is your friend?"

Roona's eyes brimmed with tears and she hadn't even eaten pie. "This is Gideon. He moved in next door to us."

"Are you the same age as Roona?"

I nodded.

"You'll be at the middle school in the fall, then?" Miss Oberman asked.

I nodded again, but couldn't find my voice. My

mother would say it was rude not to answer, but I just couldn't. My head was too busy trying to deal with the fact that Roona's fears about her mother's sad blueberry pie had maybe, possibly come true. I'd seen it with my own eyes, or I'd never believe it even as a *maybe* possibility.

Mrs. Oberman made a noise and I was saved when her daughter went to her. She said, "You kids better get going now."

I wiped at my eyes.

"Yes, ma'am," Roona said again. And we left.

Five

I didn't see Roona for the next three days, during which I actually did start to read *The Hobbit* for the seventh time. I got as far as Gandalf showing up for Bilbo.

I am looking for someone to share in an adventure that I am arranging, and it's very difficult to find anyone.

I avoided her, because frankly between the movie with her mother and the crying at the old folks' home, I was a little freaked out.

I did watch her through my window, skating on her porch. If her father hadn't shown up in twelve years, it didn't seem like he'd show up on a random afternoon just because she was waiting. But she was out there, every day.

For the first time, I had a secret I couldn't tell my parents. Not a silly little secret. A real big whopper of a secret.

They thought I'd been next door playing with Roona, when really we were miles away, chasing down a possibly magical blueberry pie. Every time I thought about it, my stomach hurt.

"That's it, Gideon," Mom said after lunch on the third day. "Get dressed."

"Mom . . ." I held up my book. "I'm reading."

"You're coming with us."

"Where?"

"To Harper's new school."

I sat up and frowned. "It's June."

"The PTA is holding a meeting for kindergarten families."

"Why do I have to go? Can't I just stay here? I'm almost done with my book and—"

"Get dressed, Gideon."

The real reason Mom made me come to the school with her became obvious about three minutes after we walked in the door. The parents all sat in chairs at one side of the room. The kids were gathering around lunch tables on the other.

She stopped at the door and I saw her take a breath. For the first time, it occurred to me that she was in as new a situation as I was—and she didn't know any more people than I did. She looked at me and said, "Keep a good eye on Harper for me."

Uh-huh. I looked around for somewhere I could sit and read, and still make sure my little sister didn't burn the place down.

"Come on, Giddy." Harper took my hand and walked toward a group of girls sitting around a cafeteria table with a pile of coloring pages and buckets of markers and crayons. I followed, because I didn't have anything better to do.

Literally, nothing.

I could read at that table just as well as anywhere else, and maybe Harper would be occupied with new friends and leave me alone for a while.

But I smelled trouble before I saw it. Fresh chocolate chip cookies. The scent was undeniable. Like our house when Mom baked for Christmas, only better. Much better.

A lady carried a plate over and set it in the center of the table where Harper was just settling herself between two other girls.

They practically dived for the cookies. I grabbed Harper's arm before she could take a bite.

"Let me go," Harper said.

"Wait a minute." I looked around for Mom and saw her talking to a lady wearing jeans and a Logandale Lions T-shirt. They each held a cookie with a big bite out of it.

The lady who'd brought the cookies was fussing with one of the little girls, tucking stray ends of her hair into a ponytail.

"Excuse me," I said. "Did Mrs. Mulroney bake these?"

"Oh yes. Make sure you get one. You'll never taste a better cookie."

"Oh no." The cookies weren't blue, of course. Maybe it wouldn't be so bad. Maybe the cafeteria wouldn't fill up with tears and my little sister wouldn't float away—

I looked back at Harper. She'd picked up a second cookie in her other hand and smiled at me through a huge bite. I let go of her.

It started with some kids who found the musical instruments stored along the back wall.

One boy, with chocolate smeared around his mouth, banged on a huge bongo drum, and another found the xylophone mallets and went at it like a maniac. They both whooped and hollered. Two women came running toward them, probably their mothers.

"Aiden, you stop that," one of the women said. "Stop that right this minute!"

The kid with the mallets played harder.

Another group of five-year-olds started fighting over the dress-up clothes that someone had set up near the milk cooler. Before I could figure out what was happening there, though, a purple marker hit me smack in the center of my forehead.

All of a sudden the room exploded in flying markers and Legos and princess dresses, screaming little kids, embarrassed parents, and reprimanding teachers.

I stood in the center of it and noticed: everyone had a cookie. Everyone. Including my mom, even though I was pretty sure those cookies were full of gluten.

I didn't really believe that Mrs. Mulroney baked what she was feeling into her cakes and pies and . . . apparently, cookies. No one could do that.

But the PTA meeting was going off the rails and everyone was eating the cookies. If what Roona said was true, what was her mother feeling when she baked these?

"Where's your sister?" Mom asked me as she shoved the rest of the cookie into her mouth. I had never seen her shove anything into her mouth before.

Quintons had notoriously good table manners.

Harper was under the coloring table with two other girls, shooting crayons at people's ankles like poison darts. They had a plate of chocolate chip cookie crumbs between them.

Mom reached under the table and grabbed Harper by the arm. "Have you lost your mind?"

Harper screamed and went loose, slipping out of Mom's grip and collapsing at her feet. Maybe she got away with more than I could, but she was also small enough to be picked up and carried out of the cafeteria. She reached over Mom's shoulder toward another little girl who was being carried in the opposite direction by her mother.

"Isabella!" Harper moaned. "I want Isabella."

"Harrrperrr!" the other girl cried. Only it came out Hawwwpawww. That kid was definitely going to be in Speech when school started.

"You stop that right now, Harper Marie Quinton." Mom grabbed my arm with her free hand as she walked past me and hustled us both toward the door. "Right this minute."

We went outside. Harper called out for the other little girl again, then slumped against Mom's shoulder.

Once my sister was buckled into her booster seat, Mom leaned in and said, "I certainly hope, young lady, that I didn't just see an example of how you plan to behave when you start school."

She walked around the car and got in. She waited for me to buckle myself up before starting the engine. She didn't pull away from the sidewalk, though. She turned over her shoulder and looked at Harper. I looked, too.

Harper's bottom lip quivered. "I want to play with Isabella."

"I have never—" Before Mom could finish her sentence, the school door burst open and two dads came out, each one holding a little kid by the arm. The two men were yelling at each other over the tops of their kids' heads.

Mom hit the button that locked all of our car doors with a solid *click*.

More people came pouring from the school. Teachers. Parents. Kids. I saw a mom screaming at a teacher, kids chasing one another around and around the pillars in front of the school.

And then in the distance, sirens.

"Okay, that's it." Mom put the car in reverse and backed out of her spot. Harper's head bobbed over and rested on my shoulder.

"I'm sorry, Mama," she said.

The whole way home, Mom kept saying things like *I've never seen anything like that* and *I can't believe that just happened.*

When we got home, she stopped in our driveway and just sat there, both hands on the wheel.

"Mom?"

She shook herself and cut the engine. "I think I'm going to lie down with Harper."

"Can I go to Roona's?"

"Sure," she said. She didn't even say anything about whether or not Mrs. Mulroney was home.

*R*oona came outside and shut the door carefully behind her. "Hi."

"Did your mom make chocolate chip cookies for the PTA?"

Roona covered her face with her hands. "Oh no."

"Oh yes. The *police* came. It was crazy."

Roona's bottom lip quivered and tears fell down her cheeks. "I've never seen her like this, Gideon. Not even when—"

"Not even when what?"

She shook her head and sniffed. I was angry when I knocked on the door. It would have been easy for Roona to warn me about the cookies (even though I had been avoiding her, and I didn't know I was going to the PTA meeting until my mother made me get dressed). Now she was crying, though, really crying, and I had to do something.

"What's wrong?" I asked.

Roona looked back at her front door, then took my arm and led me down off her porch.

"She didn't sleep last night. Not at all. She—"

"She what?"

"My dad's leaving," she said.

"What do you mean? You said you haven't seen him since you were a baby."

"I haven't." She bit at her bottom lip and looked at me for a long moment. "If I show you something, do you promise not to tell anyone?"

"What is it?"

"Something about my dad. Do you promise?"

I wondered if I needed to call *my* dad at work. This day was getting seriously weird.

"Well," she said, "do you?"

"Fine. I promise."

Roona spit in the palm of her hand and held it out to me. I took a step back. "What are you doing?"

She waggled her fingers. "Come on. Spit swear."

"Ew."

"I'm serious. Spit swear, or I can't show you. Just do it."

I sighed and looked at her spit-slick hand. "Fine."

I spit in my own palm and winced as I pressed it against hers. "This better be good."

She let go and I wiped my palm on my pants. "Wait here."

She went inside her house, and a minute later came back with an envelope. "I found this."

"What is it?"

"A letter from my dad." She held it against her chest for a minute, then out to me.

I took it and looked at the envelope. It was addressed to Miranda Mulroney from Curtis Mulroney. The return address said Nellis FPC, a long number, and a Las Vegas address.

"Nellis," I said.

"That's the air force base."

I opened the envelope and pulled out a folded sheet of paper. It wasn't a very long letter, only a couple of lines scrawled across a sheet of plain white paper.

They're moving us to Moriah. I'm sorry, Miranda. I'm so damned sorry. Maybe it's for the best. I'll miss you.

I turned the paper over in my hand. "That's it?"

Roona nodded and took the letter back from me.

"What's Moriah?"

She reread the letter and answered without looking up. "A little town up near the Idaho border. I Googled it."

"What's the big secret?" I was missing something. "You don't see him anyway, do you?"

That was the wrong thing to say. I knew it as soon as it came out of my mouth. Roona's face tightened as she carefully put the letter back in the envelope. "I think my mom does, though. He says right there, he'll miss her."

The letter didn't say anything at all about Roona.

"Why would he see her and not you? That doesn't make sense." I couldn't imagine my dad not seeing me and Harper, ever. For years.

"I think this is why my mom's . . . why she's not herself."

"The cookies," I said. I was still shaken by what I'd seen at the PTA meeting.

Roona nodded again. "And the pie. We have to find him and tell him. If he knew how much she needs him, he'd come. I know he would."

"What do you mean we have to find him?"

"I'm really worried about my mom, Gideon. I'm afraid that she's sick—like she was before. When she took too much medicine."

"Maybe I should go get my mom," I said. "She was a nurse before I was born. She'll know—"

"No!" Roona grabbed my arm. "You swore not to tell. You *spit* swore."

I did spit swear. I wiped my hand on my pants again. All I knew, in that moment, was that I needed to make Roona stop crying. I had to do something, anything, to help her.

"Okay," I said. "All right. But what are we going to do?"

"Will you help me find my dad?"

I knew this was bad. Very bad. I closed my eyes and could not see a way for this to go that didn't end up with me grounded until I graduated from high school. "Find him how?"

"We have to go to Las Vegas."

She might as well have said we needed to sling-shot ourselves to the moon. "Las Vegas? Like *the* Las Vegas?"

"It's not that far. Only sixty miles and—"

"Sixty miles? Are you crazy? I'm not even supposed to cross the street."

"You went to the old folks' home with me."

I laughed and hoped she'd laugh with me. She didn't. "We can't go to Las Vegas, Roona. Why don't you just call him?"

She finally did laugh then. And she shrugged, like it wasn't a big deal. Like she wasn't crying a few minutes before. "Never mind. I'll go on my own."

She held up her hands, still holding the letter, as she backed toward her house. She started up the stairs to her front door and I don't know what came over me. I couldn't walk away.

"I have a hundred dollars."

She turned slowly back to me. "Really?"

"From my birthday. But, for the record, I think this is a really bad idea."

*B*uying two Greyhound bus tickets required some maneuvering.

We rode our bikes to the grocery store first. It was about a half mile past the old folks' home, so I was breaking the rule again. It was easier this time. Maybe getting away with something always made it easier. I wondered if that was how people became criminals. I really hoped not.

I saw Miss Oberman's truck in the handicapped spot as we passed.

Mom was still asleep when I'd gone in to get my stash of money. I hoped she'd just assume I was still at Roona's, and wouldn't come looking for me before we got back.

I really did feel like Bilbo Baggins on a Tookish adventure and it was exciting to the point of making me feel dizzy.

"We need to buy a gift card," Roona said when we pulled up in front of the store. "Like a credit card, you know, that we can use to buy bus tickets online."

"Do they sell those to kids?"

She tilted her head from shoulder to shoulder. She didn't know. Neither of us knew what we were doing and I felt my stomach do a slow, nauseating flop. Roona just smiled and said, "Let's go."

I thought about going into the store with her, but changed my mind. I wanted as little to do with this as possible. It was cowardly and I knew it, but the high I'd felt riding my bike with my birthday money in my pocket did not last. My Bilbo Baggins moment faded when I realized that I wasn't prepared to follow Roona into the store.

"I'll stay with the bikes." I offered the little stack of tens and twenties I'd been given in birthday cards from my aunts and uncles and Grandma Ellen.

I had been saving it since February, in case my parents made good on their promise to take us to Disneyland. Saving it, but not holding my breath. Now I was just throwing it right down the drain.

Roona took it and said, "Okay. Wait here."

If I actually took a Greyhound bus to Las Vegas with Roona, there was no way I was ever going to Disneyland or anywhere that wasn't school or my bedroom until I was as old as Miss Oberman. Or maybe Mrs. Oberman.

$\mathcal{R}$oona came back ten minutes later. She got on her bike without saying anything.

"Did you get it?" I asked. She started to pedal away, back toward our street. I had to hustle to catch up with her. "Roona!"

"I got it," she said over her shoulder. "We need to hurry."

I looked over my shoulder, too, half expecting a security guard or someone to come after us. "Why?"

She followed my gaze and then rolled her eyes. "We're not in trouble, Gideon. My mom'll be home soon. I need to order our tickets."

Crap. I was on a runaway train and all I could do was hang on and ride. I didn't think it was going to do any good, but I had to at least try to slow things down. "Are you sure this is a good idea?"

Roona pedaled faster. She wasn't wearing her baby-blanket cape, but I swear I heard an echo of it snapping in the wind.

Six

I sat on Roona's porch and watched my own front door. It was so quiet over there, I was sure that Mom and Harper were both still asleep. Roona had gone into her house, with my birthday money in gift card form, and didn't even invite me in.

My heart raced, but the honest truth was that I was enjoying this. I'd never had an adventure before. Not a real one. Driving across country and seeing things like the world's largest bottle of hair tonic was as close as I'd ever come.

This blew *that* away.

I thought about the chaos I'd seen at the school and had the strange sensation of the whole world tilting, as if I was on a ship.

Roona believed her mother's feelings baked into her cakes and pies and cookies. It seemed impossible, but I had seen the whole old folks' home in tears, and the PTA meeting gone crazy.

I couldn't say I didn't believe it, either.

When I was eight years old, Jackson Emery told me that he didn't believe in Santa Claus. I had my doubts by then, of course. But it was the first time any of my friends had ever said it out loud. It was like a soap bubble bursting—only I didn't realize it was as fragile as that until it was broken.

Roona and her mother were like that Santa bubble, only in reverse.

I didn't think I believed in magic, until it was right in front of me, fragile as a soap bubble. Maybe. And what if it was true?

What was going on with Roona's mom that made her cookies—full of her emotions—make a whole roomful of kindergarten kids and their parents behave the way they had?

What had made Roona believe that she needed

to go all the way to Las Vegas on a Greyhound bus to find her dad, instead of doing something normal like calling him?

I had just about talked myself into calling *my* dad, because I was in way, way over my head, when Roona's front door opened.

She sat down beside me with two pieces of printer paper in her hands. "The bus leaves tomorrow morning at eight."

This was too much. "I'm not even allowed to go to your house before eight."

"The Greyhound station is pretty far," she said. "We better leave here by seven. We'll have to park our bikes at the station, so don't forget your lock."

"You aren't listening to me."

Roona leaned forward, elbows on her bare knees. "I have to go, Gideon. With or without you."

With or without you. It was the refrain of my mom's favorite song. Great. I closed my eyes. "This is a bad idea. You know that, don't you?"

"I haven't seen my mom like this since—" She folded the tickets neatly. Lengthwise, hot dog–style, then widthwise, hamburger-style. "Since I had to go live in Idaho."

I waited, but she didn't go on, so I said, "What really happened in the third grade?"

She unfolded the papers, smoothed the creases, then folded them again. Hot dog. Hamburger. "I told you. She took too much medicine and I had to go live with my aunt Jane. I can't go back there, Gideon."

Everything in me tightened, like a fist. There was something under what she was saying. Something I wasn't sure I wanted to understand. "Roona."

Roona unfolded the tickets again. "She had to go to the hospital for a long time. Weeks and weeks. She can't get that sick again, Gideon. I need her. If she gets sick again, they might make me stay in Boise for good this time. And she needs my dad."

"What happened in Boise?" I waited, but she didn't answer. I looked at my house again and thought about my mom in there with Harper. "We're going to be in so much trouble."

"We'll leave notes."

Right. *Dear Mom and Dad. I took a Greyhound*

bus to Las Vegas with Roona. Don't wait up. "What
time will we be back?"

"Are you sure you want to know?"

I lifted my shoulders. "Ah . . . yeah. I think I need
to know."

"Midnight."

"Right. Of course." Actually, coming home didn't
matter much. Mom would notice I was gone about
the time the bus left Logandale. When I told my
sixth-grade teacher we were moving to Nevada, she
told me about the nuclear bombs that were tested
here in the 1950s.

The explosion when my mother realized I'd left
the house at seven in the morning to take a Greyhound bus to Las Vegas would put those mushroom
clouds to shame.

I was in a state that still felt like a geography
class footnote, thinking about doing this outrageous
thing with a girl I barely knew who may or may
not have marginal superpowers, whose mother may
or may not have done something to herself that I
couldn't even think too hard about.

I leaned back and looked up at the cobwebs in

the rafters of the Mulroneys' porch cover. "I just don't think I can do this, Roona."

"You don't have to."

I turned my head toward her. "Really? You'll stay?"

"I'm leaving at seven."

No matter what, she would probably never see me again after tomorrow, because I would definitely never be allowed out of my bedroom again once my parents learned that I let Roona use my birthday money to do this thing.

I was going to be in trouble, one way or the other.

Roona sat with her back straight, her chin lifted. She looked as unmovable as the mountains. She was going to Las Vegas—with or without me. I had to decide if I could live with letting her go alone.

Mom, queen of natural consequences, would say I shouldn't have given my friend my money to do something stupid in the first place. She'd list the choices I could have made. I could have told Roona's mother or my own parents. I could have let Roona go and not doubled down on my own poor choices.

But she couldn't see Roona's face. Even if I stopped her from going the next morning, she'd find a way and the next way might be even less safe.

"I have no idea," Mom said to Dad during dinner. "No idea *at all* what in the world happened today. I've never seen anything like it."

Dad tried not to laugh. I could tell by the way he sucked in his cheeks and didn't look directly at Mom when she talked.

"This isn't funny," Mom said. She knew his trying-not-to-laugh face, too. "We're supposed to send Harper to that school in a couple of months."

"I'm sure it will be fine," Dad said.

It was a mistake to try to blow off something Mom thought was important, no matter how ridiculous the story sounded coming out of her mouth. Dad should have known better. Mom smoothed her hand over Harper's hair and said, "We'll talk about this later."

My stomach was in knots. We had Chinese food for dinner because Mom had a headache (she said from the gluten in the PTA cookies) and didn't feel like cooking. Logandale had two restaurants. A diner called Pop Arnie's and Happy Mountain Chinese.

The moo shu pork wasn't bad, but it sat in my stomach like a brick. Harper didn't look like she was feeling very well, either, and I had a flash of inspiration. "Want to watch *Finding Nemo* with me?"

Harper and I both have blue eyes, like our mom. We turned them to her in unison and she lifted her eyebrows, like she suspected I was trying to pull something over on her.

"All right then," she said. "You may be excused after you take your dishes to the sink."

Doing something nice for Harper helped to loosen up the guilt squeezing my guts. We took the cushions off the sofa and set them up like a nest on the living room floor, then I popped the DVD into the player.

As the movie started, Harper curled close to me. She really wasn't herself. I heard Mom and Dad talking in the kitchen and I was sure Harper heard, too. They weren't yelling or anything, so I couldn't make out what they were saying, but their tone was tense.

"Am I in trouble for being bad at school?" Harper whispered.

"If you are, it won't last long." It never did. Harper was too cute to be mad at for very long. Even for me.

"I still get to go to kindergarten, don't I?"

"Definitely. Trust me."

"Will I be able to play with Isabella?"

"Just watch the movie, Harper."

I wasn't going to Las Vegas on a bus. There was no way.

When I set my alarm clock to wake me up at six thirty in the morning, it was so that I could try one more time to talk Roona out of going.

But I didn't really need the alarm. My eyes popped open at 5:42 and I couldn't go back to sleep.

Even as I stood in the middle of my bedroom, trying to decide between jeans and a T-shirt or my church clothes—because how was I supposed to know what to wear on a Greyhound bus or to an air force base—I was certain I wasn't going with her.

But, she was going, with or without me. I decided I'd better get dressed. In case.

I went with something Mom would make me wear to Grandma Ellen's for dinner: khaki pants and a button-down plaid shirt with short sleeves. I had a tie, but I decided that would be too much.

If I was going to get dressed, then I had to at least write a note. In case.

The note was a problem. I needed to write something that would keep my parents from calling the police. I couldn't tell them where we were going, or they'd be there at the bus station in Las Vegas when we stepped off the Greyhound. We'd be dragged right back to Logandale before we got anywhere near Roona's dad.

I bit my bottom lip and sat with a pen hovering over a piece of paper. Start at the beginning, I decided.

Dear Mom and Dad,

That was easy enough. But now what? Stick as close to the truth as I could. I wasn't a good liar anyway.

I'm with Roona. Please don't worry. I'll be home tonight.

By "tonight" I meant midnight. Which was technically tomorrow morning. I groaned as I read back those three little sentences. At least they'd know I wasn't kidnapped. Mom always worried about me or Harper being kidnapped. As if there were bad guys across every street just waiting to snap one of us up if we used the crosswalk.

I know you're mad, but I promise I'm fine. Roona just needed my help.

How bad could it be, to be a good, helpful friend? Before I could change my mind, I wrote *Love, Gideon (your son)*. Maybe the reminder would keep them from killing me before they could ground me.

I left the note on my pillow. If I actually went through with getting on a bus headed for Las Vegas, alone with Roona, Mom would eventually come in to make sure I was up, and she'd find it.

I put on my tennis shoes, found my bike lock (in case), and tiptoed out of the kitchen door into our backyard.

I half expected to find Roona in her Wonder Roo getup. In fact, I was prepared to try to make her leave the swimsuit and striped socks behind if she insisted on doing this stupid thing.

It was going to be hard enough for two twelve-year-old kids to get on a bus to Las Vegas alone without one of them wearing a baby blanket tied around her neck.

Or one. One twelve-year-old kid. Because I was definitely not doing this. When I came around the corner of my house to the front, though, I stopped dead in my tracks.

Roona was dressed up, all right. But not like Wonder Roo.

Her long, wild hair was wrapped in a twist at the back of her head, like her mother's usually was. She wore a blue dress and a pair of flat black shoes, a little like Harper's ballet slippers. She wore gold hoop earrings through her ears, and lip gloss.

And her blanket was wrapped around her neck, like a scarf.

"Whoa."

She fiddled with one of her earrings. "What?"

"You look—"

"Stupid, I know. But I didn't think—"

"Old," I said. "Older, anyway."

Roona was three or four inches taller than me and, dressed up, she could have been my older sister. If you didn't look too close, and didn't notice that her scarf was really a ratty baby blanket, you might think she was fourteen or fifteen at least.

"I think it'll help us get on the bus," she said.

"You mean you."

"What?"

"It'll help *you* get on the bus." She looked me up and down, slowly. "Don't look at me like that."

"Aren't you coming with me?"

"I can't. I told you."

"But you're all dressed."

I looked down and was actually startled by my dress clothes, even though I was the one who put them on. "I can't go to Las Vegas, Roona. And you shouldn't, either."

"I have to." She shrugged. "I don't have a choice."

"Yes you do. You can just choose not to do this."

"You'd do it," she said. "You'd do it for your mom."

I tried to say that I wouldn't, but I couldn't. I

would do it for my mom. The question was whether I'd do it for hers. Or maybe: whether I'd do it for Roona. Her mouth was set in a determined line that reminded me of Harper when she gets stubborn.

Roona would go without me.

The real question wasn't whether I could let her.

I thought of all the things my mother was afraid would happen to me if I crossed a street or went to the mall or stayed out after dark without her. How I would feel if Roona got lost or kidnapped or . . .

I let out a breath with a sigh. "I can't believe I'm doing this."

"Okay." She walked to her bike. "We better go then."

I looked one last time at my house. How long would it be till Mom found my note? "We better."

The Greyhound station was on the same long, winding country road as the grocery store and the old folks' home.

Logandale wasn't anything at all like Wildwood. It wasn't anything like what I imagined Hobbiton to look like, either. It wasn't green at all. But the mountains were the biggest that I'd ever seen and the cows and fields lining the road made me feel like there might be hobbit-holes just around the corner.

We rode farther than I'd ever ridden my bicycle before. Definitely farther than I'd ever been without an adult knowing where I was.

*I*t took almost an hour to get there. So long that I was worried we hadn't left early enough. We locked our bikes to the rack outside and Roona brushed her hands over her dress, then looked at me. "Ready?"

"Are you sure this is a good idea?" I asked one more time. "You should call him first, at least."

She shook her head. "I have to do this, Gideon. If you're too scared, it's okay. I'll go by myself."

She wasn't making fun of me. Riding a bus to Las Vegas without telling anyone where we were going was scary. Mom had drilled every possible bad thing that could happen to a kid alone into my head for my whole life. If Roona went alone and something happened to her, I'd never forgive myself.

Her teenage-Roona outfit worked. She handed the bus driver both of the tickets she'd printed at her house and he didn't even look up. No one looked at us twice when we got on the bus and found seats.

Roona sat straight as an arrow beside me, her backpack on her lap. She'd given me the window seat. I watched through it, expecting my parents or maybe police officers to show up any minute.

"Calm down," she said. "You're going to get us in trouble."

"I'm going to get us in trouble?" I turned away from the window. "We're already in trouble, Roona. It just hasn't caught up with us yet."

She leaned back in her seat. "Thank you for coming with me, Gideon."

I blew out a breath and sat back in my seat, too. "How much money do we have left?"

"Twenty dollars."

I exhaled again. "At least we'll be able to eat."

"We'll need that for a cab ride to the base." Roona opened her backpack and pulled out the corner of a brown paper bag. "I made sandwiches."

"I hope you didn't bring anything your mom baked."

"Don't worry." She pushed our lunch back in and zipped her pack. "I used Wonder bread."

"Did you leave her a note?"

She looked at me like I was crazy.

"You left without even leaving a note?"

"She won't worry about me."

"Roona."

"What? She won't. She won't even notice I'm gone until tonight. Your mom will tell her before then."

"Really?" A bubble of anger pushed against my ribs. "How did you even know I was coming with you? I told you that I wasn't."

She shrugged. "I knew. But even if I was wrong, then you'd tell her."

I crossed my arms over my chest and sat straight in my seat, trying to deflate that bubble.

The bus was full. I expected the people who took this trip with us to be sketchy, scary people who a couple of sixth graders shouldn't be alone with. It was a nice surprise to see how normal everyone else was.

An old man sat in front of us. A woman and her two kids took up two seats across the aisle. A man with a service dog walked all the way to the back of the bus and sat by the bathroom.

"I'm not using the bathroom on a bus," I said.

And of course, I had to go right that minute. I thought about getting off and going back into the station, but the driver closed the doors and it was too late.

The bus started to move. I sat back, clutching the edges of my seat like we were on a rocket ship instead.

"Gideon," Roona said. "Seriously, calm down."

I tried. And it worked. The farther we went without sirens or my parents flagging us down, the more I relaxed. I was going to be in trouble, but I wasn't in trouble yet. For now, even though I'd fought it, I was on an adventure with Roona.

This was by far the most Tookish thing I'd ever done. Maybe the most Tookish thing I'd ever do. Roona pulled her blanket from around her neck and held on to it, working at the edge with her fingers.

I waited for her to say something. Anything. But

she kept picking at the edge of her blanket and I couldn't take it. "Are you okay?"

She shook her head and suddenly she didn't look older anymore. She looked like a twelve-year-old girl playing dress-up in her mother's clothes.

Which was exactly what she was.

"Your mom?" I whispered.

"I should have left a note." She looked at me. "I'm scared, Gideon. What if she gets worse?"

"We'll find your dad."

"I'm scared we'll be too late."

"We won't be."

She turned to look at me. "How do you know?"

I didn't know. I was guessing. Or maybe, hoping. I said the thing my dad always said to me when I got extra worried. "Things are almost never as bad as they seem."

"Sometimes they're worse."

"Boise was worse?" I blurted out before I could stop myself. I wanted to make her tell me. Just push and push until it all came spilling out and I could finally understand what was going on here.

She didn't look sad when I mentioned Boise,

though. She didn't look worried. She looked afraid. She shifted in her seat and held her blanket closer.

I'd never held a non-relative girl's hand before. I'd never even thought about it. But I reached for hers, because I couldn't stand how alone she looked. We sat there like that while the bus left Logandale behind.

Seven

We stopped at what felt like every single gas station between Logandale and Las Vegas to pick people up or drop them off. For such an empty-looking place, there are a lot of pockets of people in Nevada.

It didn't take too long for someone to wonder why a couple of kids were traveling alone to a place my dad called Sin City.

The old man in front of us walked past us toward the bathroom, then stopped in the aisle on his way back and said, "Headed to the city?"

I averted my eyes. The man wasn't looking at me, though. He was focused on Roona. She lifted her chin and said, "Yes."

"Long way."

She gave him a half smile and nodded, then reached into her backpack for the brown bag. "Hungry?" she asked me.

The man watched us a little while longer, while Roona took out a couple of ham-and-cheese sandwiches. It was way too early for lunch, but I took one. I was happy to see they really were made on plain old store-bought white bread.

The man's fingers tightened on the back of his seat. "Got another one of those?"

The woman across the aisle from us must have had her mom antennae up, because she pulled her kids into the window seat and moved over to the aisle. "Why don't you just sit down and leave them alone?"

The man looked at her, his face clouding. "Why don't *you* mind your own business."

The woman looked like she might stand up and really start something, but her smallest child, a little boy, climbed into her lap and she just hugged him to her instead.

"So"—the man turned back to us—"got another sandwich? I haven't had anything to eat since Salt Lake City."

Roona looked at me, her mouth tightened into a hard line. Then she reached into the bag and pulled out a plastic baggie full of brownies.

"Roona," I said, startled.

She opened the bag and pulled one out. "You can have this, if you want."

The smell of chocolate flowed into my nose, and my mouth started to water, even though I wasn't really hungry.

"Don't," I muttered. "Roona."

"It's okay," she whispered as the man took the brownie and sat in his seat with a contented sigh as he bit into it. "They're happy brownies. I hid some in the freezer, just in case."

The man stood up again so he could look at us over his seat. "Thanks."

"You're welcome."

"You got someone meeting you in Vegas, then?" He took another bite. "I could, you know, stick with you until you get where you're going. Make sure nothing happens to you."

Roona opened her mouth, but I beat her to it. "No thank you. We'll be just fine."

"You're sure? It wouldn't be a big deal."

"Very sure."

The man lifted his shoulder and sat again.

I knew there was no way for a random old guy on the bus to ask a couple of kids to hang out with him in Las Vegas without coming off like a creeper.

Maybe if we weren't on a Greyhound bus and I wasn't thinking so hard about being kidnapped, he'd look more like someone's grandpa. But at the moment, the only way he could look creepier is if he was wearing a trench coat and hiding behind a tree.

I could see well enough between our seats to watch him finish his brownie, then finally doze off with a smile on his face.

I looked at Roona. Neither of us had eaten our sandwiches. I wrapped mine and put it back in her paper bag. Then I took hers when she didn't take the hint and wrapped it, too. We were going to need those before midnight.

"I had a friend in New Jersey who lived with his grandparents," I said.

Roona looked at me.

"He didn't know his mom, but he missed his dad real bad." Cody was the only kid I knew who didn't live with at least one of his parents. "I guess after his mom died, his dad had a really hard time."

"My dad isn't dead."

"I know. But the point is that his grandparents took care of him so his dad could try to get better." I wasn't sure if that part was true. Maybe his dad was just off being an alcoholic or living on a park bench or something. Or begging kids on a Greyhound bus for sandwiches. But it sounded good. "He didn't want to live with his grandparents, but at least he was safe."

"Good for him," Roona said.

"I'm saying, maybe Boise wouldn't be so bad. If, you know, you don't have a choice."

What I was worried about, but didn't know how to bring up, was that there was some reason other than the air force that was keeping Roona's father away. If he was stationed sixty miles away, it didn't make any sense at all that he wouldn't come to visit. Ever.

Roona reached into her bag and pulled out a deck of playing cards. "Want to play Jacks?"

I just stared at her until she put the cards away.

"I'm sure his grandparents were awesome," she said.

I actually didn't know. I wasn't close enough to Cody for my parents to know his grandparents, which meant I'd never been to his house. "They were good enough," I said.

"Boise isn't good enough."

"Why not?" The question left my mouth before I could stop it. I'd been taught all my life to mind my own business and not get involved in other people's problems. Something about Roona made me a serious rule breaker.

She brought out the Tookish part of me and made me wonder where exactly it had come from. Maybe my dad. He was an artist. Both of his parents and my mom's dad died before I was born. Grandma Ellen was even less Tookish than Mom.

"I don't want to talk about it," Roona said quietly. "At least not yet."

I sat back in my seat as the bus slowed and pulled into a truck stop. "It might help to talk about it."

"I know," she said. "Just not yet."

We made it the rest of the way to Las Vegas without any real problems. We didn't have luggage, so we were able to walk away while the old man was waiting for his bags.

Getting a cab was an entirely different thing.

"Can we even take a taxi?" I asked. Every Stranger Danger message my mother had ever drilled into me was going off like a tornado warning in my head. "Are the drivers even allowed to take kids without parents?"

"We'll be fine." She wrapped the blanket around her neck like a scarf again. "Trust me."

"Is twenty dollars enough? What are we supposed to do if twenty dollars isn't enough?"

"It's enough."

I wondered how we were going to get *back* to the bus station, but didn't bring that up. Roona walked directly to the first taxi cab she saw and opened the back door.

"Roona," I said. I was afraid that the taxi driver would take one look at us—a couple of kids without adult supervision—and call the police. But my only choices were to follow Roona or stand alone at the bus station while she went off in a cab without me. We were moving forward, like it or not. I got in behind her and closed the door.

"Nellis Air Force Base, please," she said.

The driver looked at us through the rearview mirror, then turned, hooking one arm around the seat back behind him. "Are we waiting on someone?"

She shook her head. "No thank you."

"Just you?"

What was it about Roona that made lies just flow out of me like water? When she floundered, I said, "Our mom was supposed to meet the bus, but her car broke down."

"She works at the base," Roona added, shooting me a look.

The driver looked at us for another agonizing moment, then shook his head. "I can't take a couple of kids."

"But we have to get to the air force base," Roona said.

"Not in my cab, kiddo." He settled back in his seat, like he was ready to wait us out as long as it took. Or maybe call a police officer. "Out you go."

I opened the door on my side and slid out. Roona waited, but not for very long. She sighed and left the cab, too.

"What are we going to do?" I asked.

"I don't know."

I looked at the row of taxis parked in front of the station. There had to be a way to get one of them to take a couple of kids. "Can you make yourself cry?"

"What?"

I looked at her. "Cry. Can you cry?"

She sniffed, blinked hard a few times, her mouth quivered—and then fat tears rolled down her cheeks.

"Wow," I said. "Wow, okay. Come on."

I took her hand and walked toward the taxis. She shuddered behind me, gasping for a breath through tears that seemed suddenly more real than they should have been.

I tipped my head and looked into the cabs until

I found what I was looking for. "Come on," I said. "Keep your head down."

I opened the back of the cab I'd picked and pushed her in. She slid all the way in, so she was behind the driver's seat.

"Hi," I said as I slid in after her. The driver, a woman about the age of my grandma Ellen, stopped trying to look at Roona and focused on me instead. "Nellis Air Force Base, please."

She narrowed her eyes and adjusted her mirror, then turned halfway in her seat. She was about twice the size of my grandma Ellen, and twice as tough-looking. "Everything okay back there?"

Roona's breath hitched as she tried to rein it in and I said, "Yes, ma'am, thank you."

"Nellis, you said?"

"Yes please." I nudged Roona's shin with my toe when she started to lift her face. She buried it in her hands.

"Everything okay back there?" the driver asked again.

"Fine. It's just—" I looked at Roona and suddenly ran out of the lie. It was just what?

"The base?" the woman asked, as if she'd guessed something that I couldn't even assemble into a lie.

"Yes please."

"Someone's waiting there for you?"

"Our mom."

The woman looked at me for another second, then put her cab in gear and pulled away from the curb.

I'd been to Atlantic City a few times, so I didn't expect to be awestruck by Las Vegas. Even in the daytime, though, the downtown area around the bus station was something else.

I craned my neck, looking at a long, covered boulevard with what looked like as many lights as there were in all of Atlantic City shoved under it. It had a zip line running along its length and I saw a nearly naked woman with a massive feathered head-dress waiting to cross the street. "Whoa."

"She's not a real showgirl," the driver said. "You can pay five bucks to get a picture with her, though."

"Is this the Strip?" I asked.

"No. It's Fremont Street." She looked back at me

when we stopped at a red light. "You aren't from around here, are you?"

"No," I said. "Our dad was . . . um . . . he was transferred here. We had to move. My sister's not very happy about it."

"I can see that."

Roona opened her backpack again and pulled out a Ziploc bag full of . . .

"Oh no," I said.

Roona opened the bag and whispered, "Give her one."

The heady scent of chocolate and caramel filled the cab. The driver lifted her chin and inhaled through her nose.

I licked my bottom lip and then took one of the brownies. "Our grandma baked them. She's a really good baker. Want one?"

The driver hesitated, but only for a second. I held the bag closer to her and she reached into it.

I should have stopped her. I actually pictured myself reaching out, grabbing the brownie—it had caramel and pecans on top and looked delicious—from the driver, rolling down my window, throwing it out.

What would happen to birds if they ate Mrs. Mulroney's brownies?

The driver sunk her teeth into the rich chocolate before I could build up the nerve to say or do anything. Her eyes fluttered closed and she made a little noise in the back of her throat. "Holy God, that's good."

Roona carefully zipped the bag up again, as if she was handling explosives instead of brownies. She looked at me and I shook my head. I whispered, "I can't believe we just did that."

"It's okay," she whispered back. "She made them on a good day, remember?"

We were moving again, but the driver's attention was only half on the road as she took a second bite. Great. We were probably going to be in an accident. "This is the best brownie I've ever eaten. Your grandma should sell these."

It smelled good, that was for sure. I inhaled deeply and actually felt better. Calmer. I watched the meter tick away at my last twenty dollars as we drove.

When it reached $18.45 I asked, "Are we almost there?"

The driver pointed one hand toward the road ahead. "Just there."

The meter read $19.96 when the driver stopped. Roona ran the gift card through the reader in the backseat and I crossed my fingers on both hands.

It worked. Roona opened her bag and handed the driver another brownie. "For a tip," she said.

The driver hesitated, then took the brownie.

*N*ellis Air Force Base was like the building version of a T. rex. Massive. Scary. Man-eating. Roona fiddled with the edge of her blanket and looked up at the guard station.

A soldier who was the T. rex version of a man watched us.

"Okay," she said, but she didn't move except to wipe the back of her hand over her eyes. "Okay."

"Roona?"

She looked at me. "What if he's not here?"

"You're just thinking about that *now*?"

"What if he doesn't want to see me?"

I shook my head. I couldn't believe I was going to have to be the one to push us into this. "We don't have money to take a cab back to the bus station. We're doing this."

She finally started to move. The guard held a hand the size of a baseball glove out to stop us. We both froze where we were. Anyone would. The guard was twice as big as my dad and glared at us like we were the enemy.

"How can I help you?" His voice didn't match his size. It was soft and kind.

When Roona didn't answer right away, I elbowed her. She jumped a little and said, "I'm looking for my dad."

The guard raised his eyebrows. "Is he stationed here?"

"Yes, sir. His name is Curtis Mulroney."

"Is he expecting you?" Roona nodded, and I hoped my nerves didn't show on my face. "Was that a cab that dropped you off?"

"Yes, sir."

"Alone?" The guard looked around like maybe a grown-up might materialize somewhere. Roona pulled her pack off her back and dug into it, then pulled out the letter. She handed it over.

The guard didn't open it. He read the envelope and then looked like someone had punched him. The color went out of his face. He looked at us for another minute, then went back in his booth.

When he came back he held two water bottles. He handed one to me and one to Roona. I opened mine right away and drank from it. Roona just held hers.

"What's your name?" the guard asked her.

"Roona Mulroney."

They both looked at me and I said, "Um. Gideon Quinton."

"Roona, your dad isn't stationed here."

"Yes he is. Look at the envelope. He sent that last week. He's here. I want to see him, please."

"Do you kids live in Las Vegas?"

Roona clamped her mouth shut, but I was already shaking my head. I stopped. The guard looked down his nose at us, then said, "Stay right there."

He went back into his little room and picked up a telephone. He watched us through the window while he talked and I swear, his eyes glued me right there to the sidewalk where I stood. I couldn't have run if I wanted to. Or if I had somewhere to go. Nellis Air Force Base is in the middle of nowhere. It didn't matter that we had no money for a cab back to the bus station, there weren't any cabs anywhere near here.

"He's calling my dad." Roona wrapped her arms around her body, and even though it was so hot I felt like I might melt into the ground under my feet, she looked cold. "Right?"

"Maybe," I said. It was the best I could do.

The guard hung up the phone and just stood in his little shack, staring at us for a minute, before he came back out.

"Is he coming?" Roona asked. "I want to see my dad."

The guard's mouth flattened and he held his head like he was being careful not to nod it or shake it. "We're just going to wait here for a few minutes."

Roona rubbed the edge of her blanket. "But he's coming."

The guard looked over his shoulder, at the buildings behind him. A big black car came toward us and his whole body relaxed. "Here she is."

"She?" Roona said.

The car drove up to the closed gate and the guard left us to go open it. It pulled up in front of us and the driver cut the engine, then opened the door.

A woman got out. She was dressed in a dark blue uniform. She was old, although not quite as old as Miss Oberman, and she had a kind face. Something tight inside me relaxed as soon as she looked at us.

"My name is Christine Farley," she said. She didn't come too close, didn't try to touch either of us. Just waited.

"I'm Roona Mulroney. I just want to see my dad. Curtis Mulroney. He's here. I know he's here."

"He's here," Mrs. Farley agreed.

"I want him." Roona's voice cracked and tears ran down her face. I didn't remember taking her hand, but I was holding it anyway.

"Roona," Mrs. Farley said. "Where's your mother?"

"At home. She's . . . she's sick. We need my dad."

"Where is home?"

"I want my dad." Roona's voice started to rise.

"Logandale," I said. "We live in Logandale."

Mrs. Farley nodded slowly. "You've come a long way. Are you Roona's brother?"

I shook my head. I was in so much trouble. I couldn't even imagine how much trouble.

The woman took a breath and after she released it said, "Roona, your father is here, but he's not in the air force."

"Yes he is."

"We need to call your mother." She looked at me. "And yours."

Roona pulled her hand out of mine and took the blanket from around her neck. "Why can't I see my dad? I want to see my dad."

Mrs. Farley rubbed her hand over her mouth and looked at the guard, then back at us. "Your father is an inmate at the Nellis Federal Prison Camp."

Roona froze. "Prison?"

"Yes."

"That's not true. You're lying. I have a letter. He's in the air force." Roona pulled the letter out of her backpack. "You're moving him to Moriah and now you won't let me see him. Why won't you let me see him?"

"May I?" Mrs. Farley asked. Roona thrust the letter at her. She looked at the envelope, then pointed to the return address. "Here. Nellis FPC. Federal Prison Camp. And this is his inmate number. I'm sorry, Roona."

Mrs. Farley and the guard looked at each other and I had the sudden idea that neither of them spent much time dealing with children. The scales tipped and I was suddenly less afraid of my parents than I was of being sixty miles away from them, standing alone with Roona in front of an air-force-base-slash-prison. I was only four years old the time my mom left me at the gas station, but I suddenly remembered what it felt like sitting alone in the sheriff's office eating that Happy Meal.

I felt alone then, and I felt alone now. And just like then, I wanted the one person I knew could make this better.

I cleared my throat and said, "I want to call my mom."

Roona looked at me and her face crumbled.

Eight

It took an hour and a half for my parents and Mrs. Mulroney to get to Nellis Air Force Base. My parents arrived in our SUV with Harper in her booster seat in the back. Roona's mom followed in her yellow VW bug.

Mom's teeth were clenched, her eyes red rimmed. She pulled me against her as soon as she saw me, then pushed me away and held on to my shoulders. "Don't you ever, ever do that to me again. Do you hear me?"

I nodded, but I was looking at Dad. He was wearing a button-down shirt with the sleeves rolled up, and the purple tie Harper and I had given him for Christmas last year was loosened around his neck. He probably didn't even make it to work that morning. I'd made him call in when he just started his new job, and realizing that made my stomach hurt.

I had never seen him look the way he did. He'd been crying. He didn't look angry or relieved. He looked disappointed, and it made me feel sick to my stomach.

"I'm sorry," I said.

He held Harper in his arms. He didn't hug me, like Mom did. He just shifted one shoulder. *Call me Boss*, I thought. *Please, call me Boss.* He said, "I'm glad you're okay, Gideon. We were really worried."

Harper pressed her face against his neck. She didn't look at me at all.

Roona and I had spent the time while we waited for our parents to pick us up sitting in Mrs. Farley's office. She was an administrator, she told us, and I thought that was probably something like a principal. Her office definitely *felt* like a principal's office.

Roona had sunk into some kind of funk where I couldn't reach her. She didn't speak to me or Mrs. Farley for the whole ninety-minute wait. She didn't answer when I asked if she was okay. She didn't take the can of Coke that the guard offered her.

I drank both cans of Coke and had to pee twice. When Roona got up to use the bathroom, too, I went over to Mrs. Farley's desk. "Can't she just see him?"

Mrs. Farley looked sympathetic. "I wish that I could let her."

"Why can't you?"

"First, because it's not up to me. But also, she's a minor here alone. There are protocols for visitors, especially since we're a military base. It just doesn't work the way you want it to. I'm sorry."

I went back to my seat and when Roona came back, she handed me my ham sandwich. She didn't eat hers. She just sat and held it in her lap until her mother arrived. When Mrs. Farley asked her and her mother to come into her office, Roona threw her sandwich away.

Mrs. Mulroney and Roona came back out from the office fifteen minutes later, both of them with red eyes from crying. Neither of them looked at me and I didn't know what to say, so I just watched them walk outside.

Mrs. Farley called my parents and me back into

her office next. I walked slow, like I was being led to Smaug's lair to be eaten by the dragon from *The Hobbit*.

And then I saw Roona's blanket, folded neatly on the chair she must have been sitting in. I started toward it.

"Gideon," Mom said. "Come back here."

"Roona left her blanket." When none of the adults answered, I said, "She needs it."

Mrs. Farley picked it up and handed it to me. I hugged it against my body and wondered if it was all I had left of the old Roona. I hadn't known her very long, but it seemed to me like she would never be herself again.

I wished that Roona had left a couple of the happy brownies for my parents. It was going to be a long drive home.

"*I* don't even know what to say to you," Mom said half an hour later as we drove away from the air force base. "Do you know how worried we've been?"

"I'm sorry," I said. And I meant it.

"What were you thinking?" Dad asked as he

drove with both hands on the wheel. He didn't look at me in the rearview mirror.

"I didn't want Roona to go by herself."

"If you were worried about Roona, you should have talked to us," Mom said.

I slumped in my seat, still holding on to Roona's blanket. It didn't give me any magic power. I wished it could speed up time so we could just be home already and I could be sent to my room. We followed Roona and her mother all the way home and I wondered what was happening in their little car.

I started to go to my room as soon as we got home. No need to be told. Mom stopped me, though. "Not so fast, Gideon."

I stopped and turned toward my parents. They stood together in the middle of the living room. Harper stood between them and me.

"Go to your room, Harper," Dad said.

Not fair.

"What did I do?" Harper asked.

"Nothing, honey. We just need to talk to your brother."

She pouted, but walked to her bedroom.

I held on to Roona's blanket more tightly and asked, "Can I take this next door?"

Dad shook his head. "Don't even think about it."

"But she needs it."

"Give it to me." Mom held out her hand. I held on tighter. "Now, Gideon."

I gave it over. "It's really important to her."

"I'll make sure she gets it."

Mom folded the faded pink blanket and my breath caught in my throat. It was just a blanket. A worn-out baby blanket. It didn't have any magic in it at all. Neither did the blueberry pie or the cookies at the PTA meeting or the brownie Roona gave the man on the bus.

Magic wasn't real. And I was an idiot. "I'm sorry."

"I bet you are," Dad said.

I squirmed. He thought I was sorry I got caught. And he was right. I *was* sorry I got caught, even though I knew it was coming right from the beginning. But I was also sorry I made him cry. Sorry I made Mom worry. Sorry that I'd never believe in magic again for the rest of my life.

"Seriously, I don't even know what to say to you," Mom said. She looked toward me, but not really at me.

"I couldn't let her go alone."

I didn't expect that to work, so it came as a complete shock when Dad's face softened for the first time since he showed up at Nellis Air Force Base. Mom looked at him, then me again, then shook her head and walked into the kitchen with Roona's blanket.

"Do you know the things that could have happened to you, Gideon?" Dad sat on the sofa, like the strength had gone out of him. "I've never been so scared in my whole life."

"I'm okay."

"A thousand things could have happened."

But they didn't. I wanted to say that, but I thought better of it. "I didn't mean to scare you."

"What did you think would happen?" Mom asked from the kitchen. "How did you think I'd feel when I found that note?"

Anger spiked in my guts, out of nowhere. Before I could stop it, it came shooting out of my mouth. "I said I'm sorry. Anyway, it's not like I've never been out on my own before!"

"What are you talking about?" Dad asked. Mom's face froze. She shook her head once, then closed her eyes.

Mom pushed her glasses to the top of her head and wiped her eyes.

She still wouldn't look at me and it made me angry. "I spent a whole day with the police when I was four."

"Don't be ridiculous," Dad said.

Mom sat on the sofa next to him. She finally did look at me then. And she looked like I'd reached out and slapped her. "You can't possibly remember that."

"What?" Dad looked at her and I felt like the world's biggest rat. For most of my life it had been our secret and I told. "He can't remember *what*?"

"When Dad was so sick," she said. "Remember, Gideon and I went to Philadelphia?"

"She left me at the gas station," I said. It just burst out of me. Like pus from a popped zit. "She *forgot* me. And I was fine. And I was fine today, too!"

"You left him at a gas station?" Dad stood up.

"My dad was dying," Mom said. Dad held both hands up to stop her. "I should have told you."

"Go to your room, Gideon," he said.

"Dad—"

"Just go." He looked at me, avoiding Mom. "It's fine. Just go."

I'd ruined my family. I lay on my bed and covered my face with a pillow. I'd ruined *everything* with my big mouth.

My parents would get divorced. Mom would have to be a nurse again. Harper and I would only see Dad on weekends, like my friend Frankie in Wildwood. Or maybe they'd have a big court fight, because Mom forgot me at the gas station. Maybe Mom would be arrested and go to jail like Roona's dad.

I jumped off my bed like it had bitten me and went back into the living room, ready to beg my parents to stay together. I stopped dead at the end of the hallway.

My parents stood in the middle of the room. Dad had his arms around Mom and her face was buried against his shoulder. He brushed his hand over her hair and whispered something I couldn't quite hear.

Okay, I thought. *Okay*. And I went back to my room.

*M*y whole family felt like it was running in slow motion. For the rest of the day, neither of my parents brought up my Las Vegas adventure. Even Harper was way less hyper than usual.

"Did you give Roona back her blanket?" I asked Mom while she made dinner.

"Not yet."

"Can I?"

She stirred rice into water. "I'll do it later."

"She really needs it." I couldn't stand to think of Roona next door, alone with her shaky mother, without her blanket.

"She wouldn't have left it if it was that important to her."

I couldn't stop thinking about Roona and the look on her face when that woman told her that her dad was a prisoner. Mom was wrong. She had it backward. Roona wouldn't have left her blanket if she was okay. "I just want to make sure she's—"

"I'm sure she's fine."

"I don't think she's Wonder Roo anymore."

"What?" Mom put the lid on her pot and turned to look at me.

"Can we go together to give it to her?"

She looked at me a minute, then sighed. "Fine."

She set the timer on the microwave for twenty minutes for the rice, then walked out to the living room. Roona's blanket was on the table by the door.

"Keep an eye on the rice for me?" she asked my dad. He was sitting on the sofa with Harper. The Disney Channel was on, but it didn't seem to me like they were watching it. He lifted his chin and we left.

*W*hen Mrs. Mulroney opened the front door, neither of us said anything. Her hair was the same color as Roona's, dark brown, with the same thick curls. Every other time I'd seen her, it had been pulled back in a knot behind her head. Now it was loose and sticking up all around her head in a cloud.

Her eyes were dull. She seemed to see us, but not know who we were or why we might possibly be standing at her front door. She wiped at her runny nose with the back of her hand and finally focused on Mom.

"Daria," she said. "Roona has . . . well, she has a mind of her own is what. She gets an idea in her head and it just sticks."

Mom looked concerned. She had her nurse face on, and suddenly I was scared. That face meant something was really wrong. "Is Roona here?"

"Oh yes. She's not leaving here for a good long time," Mrs. Mulroney said.

"Gideon picked up her blanket this afternoon." Mom lifted it toward Mrs. Mulroney.

She reached for it and as soon as her fingers closed around the soft, pink fabric, she started to cry. Mom handed me the blanket and said, softly, "Gideon, why don't you go find Roona and give this to her."

I took it, but was a little afraid to move. Like maybe it was some kind of trick. When both women just looked at me, I sidled into the house and then moved quickly toward Roona's bedroom.

She was sitting on the floor, under her window, curled up with her knees hugged to her chest in a patch of sunlight like a cat.

"Roona?"

She looked up at me. "What are you doing here?"

I held out her blanket. "You left this."

"I don't want it."

I'd only known Roona for a week, but the idea of her giving up on Wonder Roo made me feel weirdly off balance. "Are you sure?"

She sat up, crisscross applesauce, and said, "Wonder Roo is full of shit."

My eyebrows shot up. The curse word coming out of Roona's mouth tickled something inside me. Laughter bubbled up and when I tried to hold it back, it choked me.

"Don't laugh at me!" She stood up.

"I'm not."

"Yes you are!"

I swallowed, trying to get myself under control, and thrust the blanket toward her. "Please take it."

She'd twisted her hair into two braids, like the first time I'd seen her on her porch. Her face screwed into an angry mask. I took a step back, expecting her to scream or come after me to push me out of her room or something.

Instead, she reached up and took the blanket from me. "Fine."

My internal Mom radar told me that my name was going to come from the living room any second. "Is your mom okay?"

"No, she's not okay."

I didn't know what to say to that. My parents had never, ever not been okay. I'd never once worried about them the way that Roona must have been worried about her mom right now. Even just a couple of hours ago, when I blurted out that I'd been left at the gas station, my worry only lasted a few minutes.

"What are you going to do?"

She shrugged and shook her head. "I don't know. I can't do anything, I guess. Can I?"

Her father was in a federal prison camp. Her mom was sick in a way that I couldn't really wrap my head around. Something bad had happened in Boise, which should have been a safe place. I felt absolutely helpless. "Should you call your aunt?"

Roona shook her head. "No way."

She hugged the blanket and rubbed one edge between her fingers.

"Gideon, it's time to go." Mom's voice came from the living room. Her calm voice. The kind she'd use when Harper smashed her thumb in a door or I had a bad day at school.

"Are you okay?" I asked Roona.

She shrugged one shoulder. She had her blanket hugged to her with both arms, and that made me feel better.

Nine

I set my alarm clock for three a.m. and tried not to think too much about the trouble I would be in if either of my parents woke up and found me on the computer in the middle of the night.

At this point I was already in so much trouble that a little more seemed like no big deal. What were they going to do?

I thought it would be hard to sleep, but when my alarm went off, I was deep in a dream about being on that Greyhound bus with Roona. Everyone in the other seats sat frozen, like people in the wax museum we went to last summer. Even Roona. The bus drove on and on through the desert and I was the only one who noticed.

I stumbled into the living room, groggy, tempted to just go back to bed.

But I had to know.

Our computer was on a small desk under the window. It was the same in Wildwood. Dad liked to look out when he worked there. I glanced over my shoulder at the hallway, half expecting one of my parents to be standing there. Then I turned on the monitor.

The computer let out a little three-note blurt and I nearly came out of my skin. I covered my own ears, as if that would help. My heart felt like it had jolted up into my head and I wasn't groggy anymore.

I looked at the hallway again and held my breath, but no one came out. I didn't hear my parents' bedroom door open. When I could breathe again, I carefully typed "Curtis Mulroney" into the search bar.

The results popped up almost instantly and I knew right away that Roona had never Googled her father's name. I'd never Googled my parents, either, and as soon as I had that thought I felt queasy. Like that time I ate a cracker with fish eggs on it at my aunt Laura's house when I was eight.

I felt like I was snooping. Like I was digging through Roona's personal, private things.

I clicked the first link and read this:

Curtis Mulroney, 25, was arrested today in Las Vegas after a three-day manhunt. Mulroney is suspected of arson. Authorities suspect the Logandale plumber of starting a house fire after a drunken argument with his wife. The Mulroneys' infant daughter was sleeping in the house. There were no injuries.

"Oh my God." I looked back at the hallway, suddenly wishing that my mom or dad would come out. It would be worth getting in trouble if it meant not sitting alone in the dark with the knowledge that Roona's father was in prison for lighting a fire that could have killed her.

I didn't know what to do. I couldn't make myself click any more links. Eventually I turned off the computer and went back to bed. But not to sleep. I didn't sleep anymore that night.

I was lying in bed, staring at the ceiling and feeling sick to my stomach, when Roona knocked on my window at dawn. I nearly jumped out of my skin.

She looked through the window at me. Her face was puffy and red, like she'd spent the whole night crying. Her hair was a halo of tangled curls. She waved one hand toward herself and said, "Meet me on your porch."

"I can't," I said. "I'm not allowed."

She pinched her lips together, then came closer. "Fine. Then open the window."

She obviously wasn't going away and if I opened the window, at least I wouldn't have to yell through it, so I did. Before I knew what was happening, though, she was coming headfirst into my room, right over my dresser. I grabbed the lamp before it crashed to the ground.

"Are you crazy?"

"I need your help, Gideon."

I put the lamp down once she was standing in the middle of my room. "What's wrong?"

"My mom's sick," she said. "Like before."

"Like when you went to your aunt's house."

She nodded and wrapped her long, skinny arms around her body. "I'm scared."

"Do you want me to get my mom?" I wanted to get my mom. Badly.

Roona shook her head. "She needs my dad."

"Roona."

"I'm going to rescue him."

I kind of half laughed, hoping she was kidding. She was not. I could see that in the way her face set, her chin lifting like she was offended I wasn't taking her seriously. My laugh turned into just staring at her and blinking. "You can't rescue someone from prison."

"Yes I can."

"The prison's on an air force base."

"I'm serious. I'm going to get him out of there. Will you help me?"

"No, I won't help you."

I expected her to get mad at me. To scream and wake up my parents. To cry. If she had done those things, it would have made sense. But she just went over to my dresser and started to climb onto it, so she could get back through the window.

"Wait. What are you going to do?"

She stopped without turning back to me and said, "Don't worry about it."

I'd been up for hours with visions of baby Roona trapped in an inferno twisting in my head. I said the only thing I could think of to stop her. "Your dad almost killed you, Roona."

She froze. She wasn't moving anyway, so it really did seem like she turned to ice, right there by my window. "Don't say that."

"I Googled him," I said. "It's true. He started that fire, when you were a baby. That's why he's in prison in the first place."

"He saved me." She went from ice to fire, just like that, and jumped back from the dresser to my bedroom floor. Her voice rose and my eyes darted to my door. "He saved me!"

"From a fire he started. Look it up yourself."

"Shut up! You shut up!" She leaned forward, her face close to mine, and then screamed, "I hate you!"

I stepped back, as if she'd slapped me. Her hands were fisted at her sides and she was shaking like it took all she had to keep from hitting me. "I'm sorry," I said.

My bedroom door flew open, and even though I knew that I was in more trouble than I ever had been, even more than yesterday—because I was still in trouble for that—I had never been happier to see my parents.

Except, when I looked up, it wasn't my parents at the door.

"Giddy?" Harper rubbed her eye with one fist and tugged at her nightgown with the other. It was too small now, but it was her favorite because she thought it made her look like a princess. "Giddy, why are you yelling? It's *early*."

Roona looked at Harper, then me again, then went over to my dresser. She climbed back out the window, headfirst. I stood on my toes to lean over and look out after her. She popped up to her feet and faced me.

"Well," she asked. "Are you going to help me or not?"

I looked back at Harper. She was all the way

awake now and staring with wide blue eyes. Maybe if I wasn't so tired, I would have been able to think of the right thing to say.

That probably wouldn't have been, "Meet me under that big tree in the back at eight."

"I have something to do this morning."

I wanted to ask, but didn't. I just said, "At three then."

Roona left.

Harper shook her head and said, "Oh no, you won't meet her at the tree, Giddy. Mom said you're grounded for *life!*"

"Shut up."

Harper jerked back. "Well, she did."

"I don't care. And you better not say a word about Roona being here." I took a step toward her. She squeaked and ran back out of my room.

As tired as I was, I felt like I was never going to sleep again. Roona, her parents, my parents, the old folks crying, the PTA parents freaking out, the bus to Las Vegas, fire . . . it all felt like heavy bricks sitting on my chest.

I lay down, though, and I must have slept because the next thing I knew Mom was calling me to breakfast. Now I felt heavy and groggy, like sleep was a wet blanket covering me.

Quintons don't lie around, though. Eventually Mom came in, opened my curtains, and adjusted my lamp (I'd put it back crooked), then put her cool hand on my forehead. "Are you feeling okay this morning?"

I wasn't. Everything about Roona and her dad and mom—it was on the tip of my tongue to blurt out that I was afraid my friend was going to do something very, very stupid. That her mother might do something even worse.

But then, Mom said, "Roona's going to be okay."

"I want to go see her. Please."

"Dad and I talked last night, Giddy. We think it would be best if you didn't hang out at Roona's house right now."

"What?"

She looked around my room, like she was seeing it for the first time. "Just for a while."

"That's not fair."

She sat on the edge of my bed and put her hand

on my leg. "I know it feels that way. But it's for your own good. I just need you to trust me."

I sat up, kicked her hand away. "But it isn't fair. Roona's my friend."

"I know, baby."

"She needs me."

"She's going to be okay, I promise. We have to let her family take care of . . ." She trailed off, waved a hand around her like what she was trying to say was a gnat flying in her face. "Everything."

I froze. She knew something she wasn't telling me. I could see it on her face. And I thought I knew what it was. The only thing that made sense. "Her aunt Jane."

"Miranda said her sister is coming to take Roona to Boise."

"For how long?"

Mom shrugged. "I don't know, Gideon, and it really isn't our business. Roona will be fine. They have a farm there."

"When is she leaving?"

"Gideon."

"What about Mrs. Mulroney?"

Mom reached for me again, this time brushing the hair from my forehead. "We can't make people take care of themselves, Gideon. That's just a fact of life."

"Can Roona come hang out here, then?"

Mom took a deep breath and then exhaled it slowly. "I need to talk to Dad about that. Maybe."

That was the best I was going to get right now. "Roona can't go to Boise. She really doesn't want to, Mom."

"No one wants to leave their parents, Giddy. No matter how bad things get."

"But—"

She stood up and walked to my door. Before she went through it she turned back and said, "Did you know that people who live there call it Boy-Sea? Not Boy-Zee."

"No," I said. "I didn't know."

What I did know was nothing like this ever happened in New Jer-sey. Nothing about this move had been what I'd expected.

*D*ad kissed the top of my head and the top of Harper's on his way out the door. In New Jersey he had to take a bus every day to work at an ad agency. He was always gone by the time we woke up and usually he didn't get home from work until after we were in bed.

In Nevada, we got to say good-bye to him and he had been home for dinner every night.

Roona hadn't seen her dad at all, not even once, since she was a baby and almost died in a fire that he started. When I couldn't sleep, in the middle of the night, I tried to imagine how that had happened.

Maybe he fell asleep with a cigarette, like my mom was always afraid my grandpa Larry would do before he died. Maybe he left the oven on, which was why I couldn't make my own frozen pizzas. But I didn't think that people went to prison for accidents.

Dad was almost out of the kitchen when I launched myself at him and wrapped my arms around his waist.

He stopped, said, "Oh," then hugged me back.

I wanted to say I was sorry, again, but nothing came out.

He put a hand at the back of my head and said, "You okay, Boss?"

Something inside me unclenched and I nodded,

suddenly embarrassed. I let go. "Have a good day at work."

He smiled, then looked over my head at Mom and said, "I will. You have a good day of summer vacation."

Ten

It felt like I was never going to have another fun day again in my whole life. Harper was happy, though. I played checkers with her. Twice.

"Let's watch *Finding Nemo*," she said when I won the second time. I never let her win. It used to make her mad, until she started winning for real sometimes.

I shook my head. "I think I'm going to read."

"Reading's boring."

"No it's not."

"Yes it is! I hate reading."

"You like when Mom reads to you."

She started to put away the game. "That's different."

At least I'd had Roona for a little while. Harper didn't have any friends in Logandale yet. I don't know what came over me, but I said, "Do you want me to read to you?"

"Really?" She looked up, the game forgotten. "*Fancy Nancy*? Or *Llama Llama*?"

I shook my head. "Just wait here."

I went to my bedroom. I reached for the first Harry Potter book, but I saw *The Hobbit* sitting on my nightstand and changed my mind.

Harper didn't wait for me. She climbed into my bed and was sitting up against the headboard. I sat next to her and opened my book.

"In a hole in the ground there lived a hobbit."

"What's a hobbit?" Harper asked. "Why does it live in a *hole*?"

"Hush . . . *Not a nasty, dirty, wet hole, filled with the ends of worms and an oozy smell, nor yet a dry, bare, sandy hole with nothing in it to sit down on or to eat: it was a hobbit-hole, and that means comfort.*"

"Worms are gross."

I would have missed it, if Harper hadn't fallen asleep with her head on my shoulder. I was looking out the window because my eyes were too tired to read anymore.

Roona walked by in her teenage-Roona getup.

I sat up so fast that Harper woke up. She blinked and said, "Is the story over?"

"Stay here."

I stood and went to the window. Roona walked into her garage. To her bike. I looked back at my door. Mom was in the living room. Between Mom and Harper, I was going to have to take my chances with my sister. "Can you keep a secret?"

She wrinkled her nose. "What kind?"

"Not a bad one. I just need to talk to Roona."

She took a breath, let it out slowly, then asked, "Are hobbits good at keeping secrets?"

"The best."

"Will you read to me more later?"

"Sure," I said. "I promise."

"Okay."

I went out the window as quietly as I could.

By the time I got around to her, Roona was on her bike at the bottom of her driveway. I stood in front of her, hands out just like the guard at the air force base had done. "Where are you going?"

"To the grocery store."

"What?"

"Go home, Gideon." She tried to push her bike around me, but I put my palms on the handlebars. "Move."

I didn't know what to do. My stomach hurt, my head hurt. I felt tears just behind my eyelids and I fought desperately to keep them in. "What are you going to do?"

"I'm going to save my dad."

"How?"

"Don't worry about it." She pushed her bike around me and walked it down to the sidewalk.

I think what freaked me out the most was that I couldn't imagine what she was going to do. How could a twelve-year-old girl break a grown man out of prison with nothing but a baby blanket, a bike, and a pair of roller skates?

I looked back at my house. Harper must have kept her promise. Otherwise Mom would be dragging me inside by now. Roona put a foot on the pedal and started to swing herself into the seat.

I ran after her and grabbed the back of her dress. "Wait."

She stumbled and put her foot back on the ground. "What are you doing?"

"Can't you . . ." What? Can't she what? "Can't you just say what you're going to do?"

"Why?"

I tightened my fingers around the handful of her dress. "You can't take the bus to Las Vegas again."

"Yes I can."

"Where will you get money?"

Her mouth tightened as she decided whether she could trust me. I held my breath and didn't let it go until she said, "I took my mom's debit card."

She trusted me. That felt fantastic, for about five seconds. Then what she said sunk in. I let go of her dress. "If your plan is to get yourself arrested—yeah, that's a really bad, bad plan."

"That's not my plan."

It hit me all at once. She didn't have one. Except

for retracing our steps back to Las Vegas, the exact same way, she didn't have any plan at all.

She started to get on her bike again.

"Wait. What about your mom?"

Roona looked over her shoulder at me. "She hasn't stopped baking since we got home from Las Vegas."

My eyebrows shot up. "Should you leave her?"

"I don't have a choice." She took a breath through her nose. "I don't know what else to do."

And then I heard, "Gideon Douglas Quinton, you better get your *endangered* little rear end in this house!"

I closed my eyes.

"Crap," Roona said. "Crap."

I looked at her as Mom yelled my name again. "Gideon!"

"You can't tell her."

"You can't go."

Roona was my friend. At least she used to be. We'd had an adventure together, just like Bilbo and the dwarves. But I saw her hate me right then. Instead of staring at me, she looked right through me. Then she turned her bike around and wheeled it back toward her garage.

I turned, too. Mom stood at the door, her hands on her hips, but she didn't look angry. She watched Roona walk to her house with real concern.

*I*t felt like three o'clock was never going to roll around. The only good thing was that even if Roona did go to buy a bus ticket before then, she wouldn't be able to leave until the morning.

Finally, finally, at 2:55, I found Mom working on her scrapbooks at the dining room table.

She looked up at me and wrinkled her nose. "Do you smell something?"

I wrinkled mine, too. I did smell something. Something burning, which made my stomach turn after what I'd learned about Mr. Mulroney last night. "Can I go outside?"

"I don't want you to go to Roona's, Gideon. I mean it." She turned and looked toward the dining room window. "Seriously, what is that smell?"

"I don't know."

She went to the back door and stood on the little stoop for a minute, sniffing and looking around like she might find a brushfire burning right there.

"It smells like a barbecue to me." I'd done enough sitting around all day to know that she would want me outside. She had a thing about fresh air. "Can I please just go to the backyard?"

She finally said, "Okay. But stay in our yard."

"I will."

"And if that smoke smell gets worse, I want you to come inside."

"I promise."

Eleven

"All right," I said.

Roona turned to look at me, her dark eyes wide and eager. I instantly felt bad for making her think, even for a minute, that I was going to try to help her break her dad out of prison.

"All right, you'll help me?" she asked.

I shook my head. Roona needed help. For sure. The kind that she'd get at a school counselor's office. The best I could do for her was let her talk, so I could tear her idea to pieces and let her see how stupid it was. "No. I meant—all right, I'll listen to your plan."

We were sitting back-to-back, I was on my side of the chain link between our backyards, she was on hers. I wasn't sure about her mom, but mine was obviously still not ready to even think about letting me cross our property line.

In fact, the reason I could even talk to Roona right now was because we were in the only corner of the yard that Mom couldn't see from the kitchen window. If she came outside to check on me, she'd blow her top.

I might not be able to leave our yard for the rest of the summer, Dad said when he called at lunch to see how I was doing. *You should have thought harder about the whole circus-in-Nashville thing, Boss.*

It seemed like a hundred years ago when he had pulled over on the side of the road in Tennessee and offered to find me a circus to join. At least he was calling me "Boss" again.

Roona shifted and the chain link pressed against my back when she pushed her weight into it. She didn't answer right away. I was pretty proud of myself for not gloating.

There was no way for a twelve-year-old girl to break her father out of prison. It was ridiculous to even think about it.

"You don't have to be such a jerk," she said softly.

I turned to look at her over my shoulder, stung by the hurt in her tone. "I didn't say anything."

She picked up the water gun she'd plucked out of her little pool and squirted me. The water was warm almost to the point of being hot. I wiped it off my cheek. "Hey."

"You thought it," she said.

"I'm a jerk because I *thought* something?" I stood up. "That's not fair."

She stood up, too. Her hair was a wild bird's nest around her face and shoulders, hanging down her back in a thick tangle that looked like it hadn't been brushed since Las Vegas. She had dark circles under her eyes.

Wonder Roo had really, truly left the building.

"Where's your blanket?" I asked.

"It's gone."

"Gone? What do you mean 'gone'? We brought it back to you."

"It's gone."

"What do you mean 'gone'?"

"Burned, okay. It was burned."

It took a minute for me to understand what she'd

said. I looked toward the grill sitting by her back door.

"You burned it." Not a question. The smoke smell Mom smelled inside was stronger out here. Not like a barbecue, even though that's what I'd said. Not dangerous, either, like a house fire or a wildfire. It smelled warm, like a fireplace burning in winter. It wouldn't have taken much to burn the thin little blanket to ashes.

I don't know why it hit me so hard, but tears built up and I had that kind of pinched pain under my cheekbones that always came when I tried not to be a bawl baby.

"It doesn't matter." She waved her hand at me. "Stop looking at me like that."

Oh God. It wasn't her. Of course, she didn't burn it. That blanket was the source of her magic. Would Bilbo melt down his ring? Would Gandalf throw his staff onto the fire?

She didn't burn her blanket. She wouldn't. I closed my eyes and remembered her on the bus to Las Vegas, holding on to that stupid thing like it was a life raft.

"Tell me," I said.

She shook her head, her skinny arms wrapped around her rib cage. She looked so normal, wearing a pair of pink shorts and a white tank top. No roller skates. No striped socks. No swimsuit over her clothes.

I pushed, because I couldn't help myself. I had to know. "Your mother burned your blanket?"

"Shut up, Gideon." She stood with her hands fisted at her sides, like she was barely holding herself together. "Please."

Her mother stole her magic. What kind of mother does something like that? I wasn't even sure I believed that Roona's blanket was anything more than a ratty piece of cotton, but the idea of her own mother destroying something so important to her made the ground shift under my feet.

"She made a peach pie last night," Roona said. "For the McElroys. And one for Mr. Dunn. He was my teacher last year."

My eyebrows lifted into my hairline. I couldn't even imagine what kind of damage a peach pie baked by Roona's mother could do when she was in the mood to actually light on fire the thing that was most important in the whole world to her daughter.

I felt sorry for whoever ate it.

"Geez, Roona."

"She's made oatmeal cookies and peanut butter fudge." A fine shiver ran through Roona. "Last night she made a whole bucket of granola."

I had a vision of Smaug the dragon burning down Lake-town in *The Hobbit* and thought we would probably read about the results of Logandale eating Mrs. Mulroney's baked goods online the next day. "A most specially greedy, strong and wicked worm."

"What?"

"Never mind." I put a hand on the chain link, threading my fingers through it, even though it was almost too hot against my skin. "I think we used some of Harper's old blankets to wrap dishes in. I could find you one."

Roona gave a halfhearted little laugh. She didn't have to say it. I knew. "That won't work."

"It might."

"God, Gideon. It was all pig poop anyway."

I didn't mean to laugh. In fact, I worked pretty hard to hold it in. But when she said *pig poop*, I couldn't help it. Roona stared at me, which made it worse. I shook my head, put my hands on my knees, and tried to focus on the dirt between my feet, but I couldn't stop.

"Wonder Roo was stupid. She wasn't real." She narrowed her eyes and stood there like Peter Pan, with her fists on her hips. I swear, I heard her blanket cape snap in the wind, just like when we rode our bikes to the grocery store.

"Pig poop," I gasped.

And then she laughed, too.

Finally, when we both had our breath again, we moved back into the shadow of the big cottonwood, out of the hot sun—and out of view of our kitchen window. Mom would have to come all the way outside to see that I was talking to Roona.

She collapsed with her back against the chain link and I did the same, sitting a little away from her so that we could turn our faces and see each other.

"Truth," she said after a minute.

"Okay."

"Do you ever think about dying?"

Whatever residual bubbles of laughter were left in my belly popped and disappeared. "What?"

"Do you ever think about dying?"

I bit my bottom lip and pressed my cheek against the warm metal diamonds. "I think about my grandma Ellen dying sometimes. She's old and . . ."

"And what?"

She wasn't supposed to ask another question, but I answered anyway. "I think she's sick, but no one talks to me about it."

Roona pulled her feet up, so her knees were under her chin, and leaned back against the fence. "I'm sorry."

I waited a minute, but when she didn't answer her own question, I prompted her. "Do you?"

"All the time."

I squirmed a little. I'd never talked about dying before with anyone. Especially not someone my age. "You think about dying all the time?"

She looked at me, her dark eyes searching for something. How I'd react, maybe. What I'd say. I didn't know what to say, but the silence was too much so I kept talking. "What about it?"

"Mostly about my mom. I think about her dying a lot."

"Because she almost did?"

Roona bit at her bottom lip and shrugged.

"Truth?" I asked.

"Okay."

"Did she take too much medicine on purpose, that time?"

"She said it was an accident."

"Do you believe her?"

Roona shook her head in a way that didn't mean yes or no. Then she changed the subject. "What's the worst thing you've ever done?"

I rubbed a hand over my face. "I'm probably going to be grounded until high school for taking that bus to Las Vegas."

"That's the thing you got in the most trouble for," she said. "But it wasn't a bad thing. What's the worst, worst thing you've ever done?"

I knew the answer. I still woke up from dreams about it, in a cold sweat. But *man* I did not want to tell her. I picked at the stray grass beside me and wished that I had a water bottle, because my mouth was suddenly so dry.

She didn't have the same problem with awkward

silence I did. She waited me out until I finally said, "I almost let Harper . . . I mean, I think she was almost . . ."

I couldn't say it out loud after all. Roona sat up straighter, and her dark eyes went round. I tried again.

"I was supposed to watch her at the park while my mom was on a phone call, but my friends showed up and I ignored her."

"Ignoring your sister is the worst thing you've ever done?"

My face burned, hotter than even the sweltering afternoon could account for. I'd never told anyone. I was pretty sure even Harper didn't know. "I saw some guy talking to her. A grown-up."

"A stranger?"

"Yeah."

She covered her mouth with her hand. "God. But nothing happened, right?"

"I called her name and she ran to me. The guy got in his car and drove away."

"Did you tell your parents?"

I shook my head. "I've never told anyone. None

of my friends saw. I don't think Harper knew what was going on, or she definitely would have blabbed."

"Holy crap, Gideon."

"Your turn," I said. This was the point of her question. She had something she wanted to tell me and I was suddenly angry that she didn't just *say* it without making me remember that man bending down on one knee, talking to my sister on her level.

Roona leaned her head back against the fence. Her wild hair poked through the links. "I was glad."

"Glad for what?"

"That day, when I came home and my mom took the medicine . . . the day I had to call 911."

That didn't make sense. "Why would you be glad for that?"

"I thought my dad would come home, for sure. I thought he'd come take care of me." She wiped the back of her hand across her nose. "I thought, finally. He'll come home and my mom won't be so sad all the time."

"Geez, Roona."

She stood up and brushed her hands over her shorts. "Yeah, well. Whatever. He didn't come home.

Guess he couldn't, right? Who knows if he would have anyway."

"I'm sure he would have." I wrinkled my nose. Lame. "If he could have."

"He almost killed me." She shook her head and walked toward her house.

I stood up, too, and put my hands on the fence. "Truth?"

She turned back to me. When I didn't say anything right away she lifted her shoulders. "Go."

"What would happen if your mom baked a pie right now? I mean, what would happen if we ate one of the pies she already baked? Or, you know, the cookies or fudge or whatever."

She ran a hand through her hair. Her fingers got stuck in a tangle and she winced as she pulled it out. "Nothing. Nothing would happen, Gideon. Pie is just pie."

I clenched my fists at my side. "You don't believe that."

"Yes. I do."

"Then pretend you don't. What would happen if we ate one of those peach pies?"

She stared at me for a minute, turned away from me, took two steps, then stopped. She came back and threaded her fingers through the fence. "We'd cry. We'd cry so much, it would flood both of our houses."

"Like with that kid's birthday cake."

She shook her head. "We'd want to drown in it, Gideon."

"She's that sad, about your dad?"

She took a breath. "Not sad tears. Scared tears."

I didn't know what to say to that. She finally went inside her house.

"So." I poked at my broccoli and kept my eyes on my plate. "Maybe we should invite Roona and her mom over for dinner."

"No." Mom spooned more fiesta corn onto Harper's plate. My sister hadn't eaten the first serving. She never ate anything with green peppers in it. Even I knew that.

"Give it to Giddy," Harper said. She put her hand over her plate. "I don't want more."

"Mom—" I said.

"Jason, tell him."

"They're our neighbors." Dad took the spoon from Mom.

"Las Vegas," Mom said. "They went to *Las Vegas* on a Greyhound bus. Alone. Do you know what could have happened to them?"

"Nothing happened," I said.

"He could have been kidnapped. Or he could have gotten lost. Or . . . or . . . he could have been *kidnapped*." She sat back in her chair. "I just started letting him go into the men's room alone. None of this is okay."

"Daria."

"No. No, don't *Daria* me. He never would have done anything like that on his own." She took the spoon back from Dad and spooned fiesta corn onto my plate. "Tell me you wouldn't do something like that on your own."

She was right. I wouldn't. But suddenly I really wished that I would. I wished it harder than I could ever remember wishing anything. I had a flash of a daydream, me telling my mom that I was exactly the kind of adventurous kid who would take a Greyhound bus to Las Vegas to help a friend.

It made me feel better, absurdly, that I had done just that. Better enough to tell her what she needed to hear. "I wouldn't, Mom."

She pointed her spoon at me. "I don't want you hanging out with Roona."

I took a bite of the corn. "She's my friend."

"You barely know her," Mom said. "You'll make friends when school starts. I promise."

I put my fork down and stood up. "Roona's my friend. You can't just tell me that she's not my friend."

"Okay, Boss—"

I left before Dad finished whatever he was going to say to try to calm me down. I didn't even take my dishes to the sink. Both of my parents gave me the most Quinton-ish looks possible. Like they'd look at me if they knew I stood up at the front of a movie theater with Roona and her mother, and sang raccoon girl songs.

"Gideon Douglas!" Mom called after me.

"Leave my endangered rear end alone!" I called back, then actually stopped in my tracks, shocked by my own nerve. I heard her gasp, but no one called me back.

I wanted to leave the house. Go get Roona and take off on our bikes. I didn't even care where. The mountains. The desert. Las Vegas. Whatever. Leave her crazy mom and my overprotective parents behind.

I went to my bedroom instead. I closed the door and leaned against it. It wasn't far enough away. I heard everything they said.

Mom said, *Don't look at me like that. You know I'm right.*

Dad said, *They're our neighbors, Daria. It's not like we can keep them apart.*

Harper started to cry. Mom probably gave her more fiesta corn. Or something.

"This sucks." I took a breath and said it again, louder. "This sucks."

Then I yelled it.

"This sucks!"

All the noise out in the kitchen stopped. And for a second I was so angry, I could hardly breathe.

I knew what they wanted.

Mom wanted me to be a *good boy*. She wanted me to do what Quintons always did: the safe thing. Pretend Roona didn't exist. That she didn't live next door. That there wasn't something pretty scary going on over there. That there wasn't some awful reason why she didn't want to go to Boise.

Dad wanted us all to get along. He wanted to tell a joke, call me Boss, and have all the problems go away.

And Harper? Harper just wanted to be a princess.

I decided to do the least Quinton-ish thing I'd ever done.

Even less Quinton-ish than the bus ride to Las Vegas or singing in the movie theater, because it was my idea.

I pulled a notebook out of my desk, and I made a plan to completely meddle in my friend's life.

Twelve

The next morning, I woke up ready to put my plan into action.

Step #1: get Wonder Roo back.

Mom kept the old baby blankets she'd used to pack breakables with in the garage. Anyone else would have taken them to a thrift store or just thrown them away. Quintons didn't waste things, though.

You never know when we might need this, Gideon.

You have no idea, Mom.

I pulled down the plastic box Mom labeled "rags" and sat on the floor with it between my legs. The concrete burned the backs of my thighs as I pulled the lid off.

I dug through until I found what I was looking for. Not the blanket with baby barnyard animals.

Not the neon-pink one. None that looked very baby-ish. No cartoon characters.

There! A plain blue blanket, faded about the same amount that Roona's had been. It was probably mine, first. That felt about right. Maybe passing it on would give it some kind of magic. All we needed was a spark.

Mom was at the grocery store with Harper, and Dad was at work. It had taken half an hour to talk her into leaving me alone and I had to move fast. I picked up the blue blanket and walked out from the stuffy heat of the garage into the burning sun outside.

I just kept walking before I could think myself out of it. Right up onto Roona's porch. I was relieved, as I knocked on the door, to see her roller skates sitting under a chair. It didn't occur to me that Mrs. Mulroney might answer the door until she did.

She looked shockingly normal. Like she'd gotten dressed out of my mother's closet that morning. Or maybe my grandma Ellen's. She wore a pink dress with a wide skirt and a white apron over it. Her hair was brushed back into a neat ponytail and her lipstick was the exact same shade of pink.

The only thing about her that looked like Roona's mother were her bare feet.

She wiped her hands over the front of her apron and left trails of flour, just as the smell of pastry washed over me.

"Gideon," she said, her voice a bit too high-pitched. "I was just . . . I'm making a pie. I thought I'd bring it over later. A peace offering. Your parents must be so upset still."

I almost choked. "You're bringing us a pie?"

"Cherry. I picked some up fresh from the farmers' market this morning."

Oh God. Oh please. "Is Roona home?"

Mrs. Mulroney opened the door wider for me. "Sure, come on in."

I looked over my shoulder, down our street. Still no sign of Mom's car.

Mrs. Mulroney had a cheerfulness about her that surprised me. Roona had made it sound like she was sad. More than sad. She sounded almost too happy when she called out, "Hey, Roo? Gideon's here."

Whatever idea I had that things were maybe okay disappeared as soon as I saw Roona.

She wore the same clothes as the day before, and as far as I could tell had probably slept in them. Her hair was a wildfire around her head and she looked like she'd spent the night crying instead of sleeping.

Her mom looked okay. Roona looked horrible.

I expected Mrs. Mulroney to do something—say something—when she saw the state her daughter was in. If I looked like Roona, my mom would have had me in bed with a thermometer in my mouth before I even knew what was happening.

Mrs. Mulroney just smiled without really looking at Roona, and went back into the kitchen. "You two go hang out in Rooma's roon—Roona's room—for a while, okay? I need to finish this pie."

Roona's face went another shade of pale and I actually stepped closer to her, afraid she was going to faint.

"She's making your family a pie," Roona said.

"I know."

"She's made fifteen pies in the last two days. And cookies and fudge and—"

"I know, Roona. You told me."

"She hasn't slept. Like, at all."

"Have you?"

She shook her head. "Not much."

We went to her room and Roona closed the door. She sat on her bed and stared at the wall in front of her. Her eyes moved back and forth, like she was reading something.

"You're freaking me out a little," I finally said.

She shifted her eyes to me. "I'm sorry. I just . . . I'm trying to figure out how to . . ."

I held up the baby blanket. "I brought this."

"That's not going to do anything."

"Yes it will."

"Gideon."

"It will if you believe it will." It really was like Santa Claus. My dad always said that everyone in our house better believe, or the stockings would be empty on Christmas morning. It was the belief that made the magic real. "It's worth a try anyway."

"It was all a big fat lie. There's nothing special about me." She sniffed, then rubbed her forearm across her nose. I shrank back from her. She really needed a shower. "I have bigger things to worry about than a stupid blanket."

Santa Claus magic. Tooth Fairy magic. Hobbit magic. I'd known that there was no such thing, right from the start. But we needed it back. We had to believe. I was convinced the only way to make any of this okay again was to figure out a way to get Wonder Roo back.

I looked around the room, hoping for some kind of inspiration. My eyes landed on the hairbrush sitting on Roona's dresser—on top of a pile of books, next to a collection of tiny little ceramic animals, all lined up on parade. I picked it up. It had ponytail holders wrapped around the handle. Perfect.

"What are you doing?" she asked.

I almost put it back down again. This was awkward and I was the worst at awkward. "My mom taught me how to braid Harper's hair."

"Okay . . ." She scooted a little farther away from me.

I sat next to her on the bed. "Just hold still."

"Gideon."

I took a handful of her hair and started to brush it, from the bottom up. I didn't have a ton of time. Mom and Harper could be back from the grocery store at any moment. In fact, my entire body was on edge, waiting to hear a knock on the door and *Gideon Douglas get your endangered rear end out here* called from the living room.

"Just hold still," I said again.

I didn't go for perfect. I just smoothed the tangles well enough so that I could put her hair into two braids, the way I did sometimes with Harper. The way her hair was the first time I'd seen her on her porch, in her Wonder Roo getup.

After I snapped the second ponytail holder in place, she brushed her palms over the braids. She already looked better, anyway. "Thank you."

"You look more like yourself," I said. I stopped myself from adding *sort of.* She needed a shower and clean clothes. And a nap. A good, long nap. But it was a start. I picked up the blanket from where I'd set it beside me on the bed and held it out to her.

"I told you," she said. "Wonder Roo isn't real."

"It's worth a try." Her mouth narrowed to a tight line and she stared at me. "Please, Roona. I have to get home before my mom does. Just try."

She rubbed her hands over her knees, then

reached up and took it. She just held on to the blanket and I didn't push harder. It was a start, I told myself again. It was something.

"We have to figure out how to stop my mom from giving your family that pie," she said. "Trust me, you guys don't want to eat it."

"Come with your mom when she brings the pie over."

"You want the pie?"

"Yep."

Step #2: convince Roona to go along with my plan.

I beat Mom and Harper home, but only by minutes. My heart pounded in my throat when I heard the car pull up before I'd even made it back to my bedroom.

I had a plan.

I didn't know how good it was, but it was something. And it was about a million times better than the idea of Roona trying to break her father out of prison.

I needed Roona to get on board with it, though. Otherwise, it was useless.

"What's for dinner tonight?" I asked as I helped bring bags in from the car. "I'm just curious."

"Curious?" Mom pushed open the screen door with her hip and looked back at me. "Salad. And I'm going to see if I can get Daddy to grill some chicken. I can't stand to turn the oven on today."

"Perfect."

Mom turned to put her bags down. "What are you up to?"

"Nothing." Salad and chicken would work. It wouldn't be hard to make it stretch to feed two more. I helped put the groceries away without being asked. Mom was onto me, I could tell by the way she kept looking sideways, but she didn't guess my plan and she didn't ask.

"Can I go outside?"

"Just in the backyard," she said.

"We should get one of those little pools, like Roona has. Harper would love it. It's so hot here."

Mom leaned back against the kitchen sink. "It certainly is. I'm not sure it's fit for human habitation. Take a water bottle with you. I don't want you to get dehydrated."

"Okay." I opened the fridge and took two. I tucked one under my arm and hoped she wouldn't notice.

"You should put some sunscreen on, too."

"Okay."

"I mean it, Gideon."

"I already did." I went out the kitchen door, into the backyard.

I was planning on throwing something at Roona's bedroom window to get her to come outside, but she was already sitting on her chair beside her pool, with her feet in the water.

My heart did something funny when I saw her. Kind of flipped over and then felt about a thousand pounds lighter.

She was wearing cutoff jeans and a yellow T-shirt, with her orange swimsuit with the green flower pulled over it. Her striped socks sat in her lap, folded on top of my old baby blanket.

Her hair was still in braids and she looked better than she had since our adventure in Las Vegas. I called out, "Is it working?"

She looked up at me and shrugged. "Hard to tell."

"I know how we can tell."

Her one eyebrow shot up. "How?"

I tipped my head toward the shade of the cottonwood tree at the back of our yards. She stood up and walked toward it.

It was cooler in the shade, but the difference between 112 degrees and 105? Not much. Having the sun off my skin, which was not covered in sunblock, was good, though.

"So?" she asked.

"We need to get my parents to invite you guys to stay for dinner tonight, when you bring over the pie."

"What?"

"We need to let everyone eat it." I took a breath. "Except us. You and me, I mean."

She looked at me like I'd just suggested we poison both of our families. "Are you serious?"

"Yes. But I'm glad you're worried."

"What?"

"It means you still believe."

"You *are* crazy."

"If everyone eats the pie, then my parents will see—"

"See what? That my mom is . . ."

"That you need help."

She shook her head. "Forget it, Gideon."

"No, I'm *serious*. I think we can talk them into letting you stay with us while your mom is getting better."

Step #3: show Mom and Dad that Roona's mom needs help.

It was going to take some doing. Because Quintons minded their own business. They didn't get into other people's problems.

The idea of letting the girl next door stay with us because her mom needed to be in a hospital—a mental hospital—to get better wasn't going to be an easy sell, no matter what.

It was going to be especially hard because of the whole could-have-been-kidnapped-in-Las-Vegas thing.

It would help if my parents could see for themselves. And it would really help if they could *feel* for themselves. That's why they needed to eat the cherry pie.

"There is no way your parents are going to let me

stay with you," Roona said. "I'll have to go back to Idaho."

"Even if that's what happens, it needs to happen," I said. "Right? I mean, we agree on that. Your mom needs help. Pronto."

Roona looked back at her house. Music was blaring out of it. Some kind of hard-driving old rock and roll. The stuff my dad sometimes listened to when he used his treadmill.

"I don't want to go to Idaho," Roona said.

"I know."

"I can't go to Idaho."

There was more to her story. Something she hadn't told me. I was tempted to call for a game of Truth. Make her spill her guts. She would, if I asked that way. Somehow, though, I knew that it wasn't the right thing to do.

Roona needed to be able to keep that one secret until she was ready to share it.

"So," I said. "Operation Cherry Pie."

Roona rubbed the edge of my old baby blanket between her fingers, then looked up at me. "Operation Cherry Pie."

"Um . . ." I bit my bottom lip, screwing up my courage to ask the next question. "If blue makes people extra sad, what does red do?"

Roona inhaled slowly. "Did I ever tell you about the time my mom made a red velvet cake for the bunco ladies?"

Oh no. "No."

Roona sat down with her back against the trunk of the cottonwood tree. "Oh boy."

I sat down, too, as close as I could with the fence between us.

"So the bunco ladies play once a month. And usually, they take turns baking something to bring. As a snack, you know?"

"Right."

"Well, about two years ago, Mrs. Neilson's daughter had a baby and she just couldn't bake her own cake. She hired my mom to do it."

"Oh God." I felt my insides clench. Like that time I snuck into the kitchen and peeked around the corner to our living room while my parents were watching a horror movie and saw someone on the screen being stabbed about a thousand times.

"She wanted red velvet. It was a mistake, of course."

"Of course it was."

"A nice vanilla or lemon cake would have been better."

"What happened? Did everyone get really mad at each other or something? Red is an angry color, right? Like blue is a sad color."

Roona shook her head. "Not angry. Mom had the Mean Reds."

"Mean Reds?"

"It's from an old movie. *Breakfast at Tiffany's.* It's Mom's favorite. The girl in it gets the Mean Reds when she's scared, but she doesn't know what she's scared of."

"I don't get it."

"When she just wants to be someone else. Somewhere else. But she doesn't know why. Don't you ever feel that way?"

I still didn't quite understand, but I nodded anyway.

"One of the bunco ladies just drove off after the meeting. She left her kids at the sitter's and never went home."

My eyebrows shot up. I really wished I could do that one-eyebrow thing. "She ran away from home?"

"Yes. The cake gave her the Mean Reds and she just left."

"Maybe she would have left anyway," I said. "Maybe it wasn't the cake."

Roona went back to fiddling with the edge of my old baby blanket. "Maybe."

"Cherry pie isn't going to make one of my parents run away from home." I wanted to believe that, 100 percent, but I couldn't stop talking. "Is it?"

"My mom gets the Mean Reds all the time. She's never run away from home."

"What happens when she gets them?"

Roona tipped her chin toward the house. Music still blared out. It was probably making my mom crazy.

"She gets lost." Roona wrinkled her face, like she was looking for the right words. "She loses herself. Like she doesn't know who she is anymore."

"She looked fine earlier."

"She didn't look like herself. She looked like a mom from an old TV show." Roona took off one flip-flop and pulled a striped sock over her foot and up her calf to her knee. She shoved her foot back in the shoe, so that the part that went between her toes pushed against the sock. "She's not fine."

"She has the Mean Reds?"

"She definitely does."

"She had them that day?" I hoped Roona wouldn't make me say *which* day. I didn't want to say it out loud. "You know. That day when you were in the third grade?"

"She had them bad that day."

"As bad as now?"

Roona took a deep breath, then put on her other sock. "No. Not as bad as now. I've never seen her like this."

"Roona?"

She looked up at me.

"I want to ask something, but not a Truth. It's okay if you don't want to answer."

She smoothed her braids back and shifted her shoulders. "You want to know what happened in Idaho."

"I get it's none of my business. Not really. But if someone knew, if we told my parents, it might make them let you—"

"You can't tell your parents."

"Roona."

"You have to promise, or I won't tell you."

I didn't like it. She was about to tell me something that a parent probably needed to know. If not hers, then mine.

I promised anyway. Because I needed to know. And because she needed to tell someone. "Okay."

"Promise?"

"Yes. I promise." She looked at me until I held up my hands and waggled my fingers to prove they weren't crossed.

She spit in her palm and held it out to me. Another spit swear. I hesitated, but only a few seconds, before spitting in my own hand and shaking with her.

"I have a cousin, Tucker," she said.

Suddenly, I wasn't sure I wanted to hear what she was going to tell me.

"He locked me in the attic closet," Roona said.

"He told me that he wanted to show me something up there."

She bent her knees and pressed her cheek into my blanket, resting on them.

I wasn't sure what to say. I expected something more. Something horrible. Being locked in a closet was bad, I guessed. Maybe bad enough. "How old is he?"

"He was fourteen when I was eight." Roona tapped her fingers on her leg, then said, "So he must be eighteen now."

"Maybe he won't be so bad this time. Maybe he doesn't even live at home anymore?"

Just like when her mother mentioned the cherry pie, the color drained from her face. I tensed, ready to call for help if she fainted. "Put your head between your knees or something."

She sat up straighter. "I'm fine."

"How long were you in the closet?"

"Until the next day."

"No one came to find you?"

She shook her head. "They didn't even realize I was gone. I mean, I was the ninth kid."

My aunt Jane has eight kids. Gertie, Amaleah, Tucker, Lola, Everett and Morgan, Harvest, and baby Joe. So many kids, she'd said the day we met, they ran out of names. "Did your cousin get in trouble?"

Her bottom lip trembled. "He didn't."

"Did *you* get in trouble?"

She nodded this time.

"What kind of trouble?"

"Promise you won't tell," she said again.

"I can't," I whispered. "I can't promise that."

She stood up, wobbled a little, and put her hand on the tree trunk to steady herself. "Then never mind."

"What kind of trouble?"

"Promise."

She stared at me and then started to walk away. I threaded my fingers through the heated fence links. If she walked away without telling me, I would be the worst friend there ever was. "Okay. Okay, I promise, I won't tell my parents."

She stopped, then bent and put the blanket on the ground without turning back to me. She pulled the straps off her shoulders and tugged the top of her swimsuit to her waist, then lifted the bottom of her T-shirt to her rib cage.

She was only a few steps away from me, out of the shade so she was in full sun. I saw the knobs of her spine, the shadows of her ribs.

And I saw two raised scars, long and narrow, running across her lower back.

For a second, I was pretty sure I was going to be sick.

When I caught my breath, I asked, "What is that?"

"She used a stick she keeps under her bed."

"Who did?"

"My aunt."

"Your mom doesn't know about that?"

She shook her head. "I don't want her to know. It will only make things worse."

She let her shirt fall, then turned to look at me. "I can't go back there."

There was more. I felt it bubbling between us. I didn't ask, though. I felt like a coward, but I couldn't take any more.

"We need to help your mom," I said.

Roona picked the blanket back up and went to her house. The music blared louder when she opened the door, then a few seconds later, it went away altogether.

"We need Wonder Roo back," I said to no one.

Thirteen

My plan was to make my parents decide to let Roona stay with us while Mrs. Mulroney got help.

Step #1 was in progress. At least Roona had a new blanket. Step #2 was done.

Step #3 wouldn't be hard. My parents knew that Mrs. Mulroney wasn't well. They just needed a little push to see how unwell she really was.

Step #4: convince my parents to let Roona live with us while her mom was getting help.

It felt like an impossible task. Like a little hobbit from Bag-End helping a band of dwarves steal their treasure back from a dragon. I didn't even want to think about it yet.

I saw the marks across Roona's back every time I

closed my eyes. I really wanted to spill the beans and tell my parents, but I knew what they'd do.

They'd call the police. The problem was that I didn't know what would happen next. Would adults believe Roona's story? If she couldn't go to Idaho, where would she go? A foster home?

No. Roona might end up in Idaho anyway. Or someplace even worse. I had to make step #4 happen. I had to. I needed my parents to let Roona stay with us. And to do that, I needed it to be their idea.

I was helping Mom make the salad when there was a knock on the door. Mom put her knife down and wiped her hands on a dish towel. "Who in the world . . . ?"

"I'll get it," I said.

I pushed around her and went for the front door.

"Hey," she said. "Gideon, wait a minute."

I threw the door open and saw Roona, still in her Wonder Roo getup—only this time with my blanket tied around her neck like a cape—and her mother standing on the stoop.

Mrs. Mulroney held the cherry pie in both hands.

"I made this for you, Daria. I just had to do something—something. I feel so terrible about Roona convincing Gideon to go off with her like that. I'm so *embarrassed*, and trust me, she's heard it from me. She'll be grounded until prom *at least*." She shoved the pie at my mom, who put her hands out to catch it before it fell to the floor. "I got a great deal on cherries at the farmers' market this morning. They're extra sweet. I think—"

"Thank you," Mom said, interrupting the rush of words from Mrs. Mulroney. She looked down at me, then took a half step back. "We were just sitting down to dinner, so—"

"Stay!" That came out of me a little too loud. Way too eager.

"Gideon," Mom said under her breath. "I'm sure Roona and her mother have plans for their supper."

"We don't," Roona said. She walked past her mother and right into our house. "Thank you, Mrs. Quinton, we'd love to stay."

"Roona—" Her mother looked as flabbergasted as mine did.

Roona took my arm as she passed me and tugged

me toward the kitchen. "Your dad's grilling, right? Let's help."

I looked back over my shoulder at our mothers, both standing there looking after us. Then I pushed Roona toward the back door.

It worked. A few minutes later, they both came outside. Harper had the sprinklers running and was standing under them with her hair plastered to her face and her shorts and tank top soaking wet. Roona and I stood at the fringe, where the mist could cool us off.

It took a couple of minutes for things to situate. Once they were in our house, or our yard anyway, there was no way my parents would say no to feeding Roona and her mother.

Mrs. Mulroney said, "I'm sorry. We should probably just go. I mean, I don't know what came over my girl. She's not usually so forward and this is your family dinner."

My dad held up his tongs to stop her. "It's okay. Really."

"I was just going to maybe order a pizza or—"

"Truly," my mom finally said, in that tone she

has that shuts down an argument in two seconds flat. She would rather not have someone in the middle of a personal crisis at her dinner table, but now that they were there, no one was going to make her be a bad hostess. "We insist. We've been meaning to have you over."

Quintons don't have a problem with little white lies, if they're polite.

"Okay," Mrs. Mulroney said. "If you're sure."

My parents exchanged a look while both mothers went to sit on the picnic bench the people who lived in our house before us had left behind.

We ate dinner on the back patio. My parents let the sprinklers go, turning our backyard into a mud pit, because it was more important to cool things off.

"I don't know how you stand this heat," Dad said.

"Oh," she said. "You get used to it. Just wait until August, you'll wish it was June again."

Mrs. Mulroney talked almost nonstop through the chicken and salad. She talked about Logandale and about Roona and about the middle school we were both headed to.

Neither of my parents spoke much at all. They kept glancing at each other. My plan was working.

"Should we heat the pie up?" Mrs. Mulroney asked finally. "I think I have some vanilla ice cream at home. I could send Roona over for it."

"Oh, I don't know—" Mom glanced at Dad.

I knew what was coming. A polite withdrawal from social duty. *Don't bother yourself. We're so full. Couldn't eat a bite of pie.*

They couldn't politely get out of serving Roona and her mother dinner, but they could skip dessert. I was pretty sure Mom wouldn't pull the gluten card. But she'd say something about Harper needing a bath or what a long day it'd been.

I stood up before that could happen. "Roona and I will serve it."

"Gideon," Dad said.

I grinned, probably too wide, and went back into the kitchen, pulling Roona with me.

The pie sat on the counter. It looked perfect. Like something out of a magazine or a commercial. It smelled wonderful, too. It would have tasted amazing hot, with ice cream melting into it. My mouth watered as I imagined the first sweet-tart bite.

"Are you sure about this?" I asked. Even though it was my plan.

Roona's face looked pale. "No."

I wasn't expecting that. I was the one who second-guessed everything, not her. "What do you mean, no?"

Cherry juice bubbled up from the little windows in the top crust, thick and red, and I was definitely second-guessing, too.

"But we have to get my parents to see that you will be better off with us," I said, trying to convince myself as much as I was trying to convince her.

"We can't feed your family this pie, Gideon." Her voice sounded sad and sort of far away. As if saying that meant she was admitting something about her mom that she wasn't really ready to face.

It smelled so good, still half warm from Mrs. Mulroney's oven, that I had to stop myself from forking in a bite right then. Roona was right. "What are we going to do?"

Roona looked at me for a long time, then took a

breath and tipped the pie off the counter onto the floor. It landed with a crash that made me cover my ears with my hands. Cherry filling splattered all over the white floor tiles, all over my feet and Roona's, and splattered the cupboard under the sink.

Before I could say or do anything, Mom was there. "Oh my God, what happened? Are you okay? Are you both okay?"

"Yeah," I said, still staring at Roona. Mom bent and ran her hands up my legs, where thick red goop stuck to my shins. "Mom, I'm okay!"

Roona's mom stood in the kitchen doorway with Dad. "I have more pies at home. Roona can run and grab one."

"No!" Roona and I said at the same time. All of the adults turned to look at us and I felt my face burn.

The energy seemed to drain out of Roona's mother. Like someone had pulled her plug. She reached for Roona and said, "We should probably start home, anyway. Let me help you clean up this mess first."

Mom shook her head. "Oh no, no, it's fine. You don't have to do that."

"Wait," Roona said. She pulled her arm away from her mother's grip. "I . . . I wanted to say that I'm sorry. I'm really, truly sorry for the whole Las Vegas thing."

Mom's mouth puckered. She was holding back whatever she wanted to say in response to Roona's apology. When she did speak, she said, "Gideon should have known better."

"I was hoping that Gideon could come to my house. Maybe tomorrow." Roona took a breath. "Please."

That last word cracked. Dad started to say something, but Mom wasn't having any of it. "Actually, no, he can't. You have no idea what might have happened to the two of you. How you would have felt if something had happened to Gideon because you decided—"

"I know," she said.

"I'm sorry, Roona. But Gideon won't be able to come play with you. At least—not for a while."

Roona nodded, then looked up at her mother.

"This is my fault really," Mrs. Mulroney said. "It's all my fault, if you think about it."

Neither of my parents argued with her.

"Maybe in a few days, you can come hang out here," Dad said. Mom shot him a deadly look. He shrugged. "Maybe."

Fourteen

After Roona and her mother left, my parents cleaned the kitchen, starting with the giant pie mess. I brought dishes in from the backyard. Harper played in the mud, which was a solid sign that things were not normal in the Quinton hobbit-hole.

Quintons did not get muddy.

"I'm sorry," Mom said. "I really am. She's a sweet girl and I feel for her. But if we can't trust Gideon to make good choices when he's with her, then he can't be with her."

"I'm right here, you know," I said.

She turned to look at me. "You're just going to have to do as I say. And trust that I have your safety at heart."

I knew she did. That didn't help. "Roona is my friend. And—"

"And what, Boss?" Dad asked.

And I thought she needed help. Like the lifesaving kind. But I'd spit sworn (twice) and if I told my parents how scared I was for Roona, I'd be breaking her confidence in a way I didn't think she'd be able to forgive.

They might not believe me anyway.

Or if they did believe me, they might call the police or—I wasn't even sure who an adult might call when a kid wasn't safe. But they would know. And if they called, then Roona might end up in Boise anyway.

It wasn't like adults always believed kids or anything.

I finally decided to tell on myself, instead of breaking my promise to Roona. "I snuck on the computer the other night."

Mom turned off the water. "I swear, Gideon—"

"Roona's dad is in prison because he almost killed her. He started a fire . . ." I watched them exchange a look. "You know."

"None of this is anything you need to worry about," Dad said. "None of it is your fault or your problem. Roona's family will take care of her."

"No they won't."

Mom dried her hands. "I talked with Miranda when we went over there to take Roona's blanket back. Roona's aunt will be here in a few days to collect her."

I clenched my fists against my sides. "Is Mrs. Mulroney going to get some help?"

"She thinks it will help Roona to be with her aunt," Mom said, avoiding my question.

I inhaled as Mom's words brought up a mental image of the scars on Roona's back. "She can't go there."

"She'll be back for school," Dad said. He glanced at Mom. "And maybe by then, it'll be okay for you two to hang out."

"She can't go there!" I reached for Dad, put my hands on his arm. "We can't let her."

"It isn't our business," Dad said, wrapping his arm around me and lowering his voice. "Try not to worry so much, Boss."

"Why can't she stay with us? Her mom—her mom needs help. She was in the hospital once, for a long time. I think she needs to go again. And Roona can stay with us until Mrs. Mulroney is better."

"I want you to go take a shower," Mom said. "And get ready for bed."

"But, Mom—"

"Now, please."

They wouldn't even consider my plan. I guess I knew that going in, but it still frustrated me. My hands tingled and I opened and closed them. I didn't know what to do—so I just did as I was told. I took a shower, then crawled into bed.

Roona woke me up early the next morning, knocking on my window. Again. At least she looked like she'd had a shower the night before.

I opened the window and she said, "My aunt Jane is coming to pick me up. For the summer."

I knew that already. "When?"

"Next week."

My heart sank. "We have to tell my parents the truth. Show them your back."

"No. You spit swore, Gideon."

"Why not? They'll do something, if they know the truth." Even as I said it, though, I wasn't 100 percent sure what that meant. What would they do? "Why is she coming, anyway? Is your mom going to a hospital or something?"

Roona shook her head. "She grew up on the farm, where Aunt Jane lives now. They moved there when she was our age. She just thinks it will be good for me."

"You need to tell her," I said. "Forget my parents. Tell your mom."

"I can't. What if it makes her like she was before? What if it makes her do something?"

Something like take too much medicine. Or worse.

"I'm going to go to Boise," she said.

I looked up. "What? No way."

"I don't have a choice."

"Yes you do."

"What is it?"

I sat on the edge of my desk. "I don't know yet."

"Well," she said. "If you think of something before tomorrow, let me know."

I looked up at her. "Truth?"

She exhaled slowly. "Sure."

I was in so far over my head. I had no idea how to even start to have a real plan, because nothing that was happening to Roona would ever happen to me. The plan had to come from her. "What do you wish would happen?"

She looked a little startled at my question. "What do you mean?"

"I mean, in a perfect world. What do you wish?"

"I wish my mom never got the Mean Reds."

"But I mean, in a perfect world, if your mom does have to have the Mean Reds, what do you wish would happen?"

She leaned against the windowsill and thought for a minute. "She'd go to a doctor and get help. But they'd probably put her in a hospital, like before. And I'd be in Boise anyway."

"Where do you wish you could go, instead of Boise?"

She bit at her bottom lip. "I don't know."

"There must be someone you wish you could stay with while your mom was getting help. A teacher, maybe? A friend?"

She took a deep breath, her dark eyes turned up to the sky outside my window, then she said, "Maybe Miss Oberman."

"The woman from the old folks' home?"

"She was my favorite teacher," Roona said. "And my mom's, too."

"Do you think she'd let you stay with her?"

Roona raised one shoulder. "It doesn't really matter, does it? My mom's not going to the hospital. I have to go to Boise and she's going to be here all alone."

Tears spilled down Roona's cheeks. I didn't think she was faking this time, like she had for the cab driver in Las Vegas. "But you can't go to Boise. Your aunt—"

"God, Gideon," Roona said. "Can't you see this isn't about me? My mom's going to be here all alone. Who's going to take care of her? Who's going to make sure she takes her medicine? Who's going to . . . ?"

Be there if she takes too much medicine. The reality

that Mrs. Mulroney could die in the house next door while Roona was in Boise with an aunt who'd beat her hit me like a truck.

"I really want to tell my parents," I said.

"All it will do is break your promise. I'll still wind up in Boise."

"Stop that!" I leaned against the window, my hands on the sill. "Just stop it, okay? Stop acting like it's hopeless. If we tell, someone will do something. They won't make you go back there."

"You really believe that, don't you?"

I did. "Yes."

"Of course you do. Your life is so perfect."

"No it's not." But compared to hers, maybe it was. My biggest problem until I met her was not being allowed to cross the street with my bike. Even now, my biggest problem was not being able to hang out with her.

"What if my aunt says that my mom hit me? My mom's sick. People will believe Aunt Jane."

I blinked. I'd never thought about adults lying. "Would she do that?"

"She's got eight kids. She's not going to just admit

to it. Anyway, what if they do believe me, and my mom gets in trouble for sending me someplace where someone hit me? What if I end up in foster care, living with someone even worse than Aunt Jane and Tucker? What if . . . ?"

"Stop!" I grabbed her arm, but she yanked it away.

She ran away from my window, back toward her house. I went out into the backyard about a hundred times that day, but I never saw her. When I threw stones at her window, she either ignored me or didn't hear.

$\mathcal{M}$om and Dad took us to Pop Arnie's for dinner.

That's what they did to try to make things feel normal. They took us out for cheeseburgers, no bun or French fries for Mom, and pretended like nothing weird or bad or scary ever happened to the Quintons.

It *was* kind of comforting.

I dipped my French fries in my chocolate shake, which was an extra treat that meant they were really, really trying to be a fun, non-weird family.

Roona said my life was perfect. She might have been right.

If something happened to my parents, I knew exactly what would happen to me and Harper. And it did not involve going to live on a farm in Boise with a creepy cousin and a mean aunt who kept a stick under her bed.

We'd go to Grandma Ellen.

And if Grandma Ellen couldn't take care of us, we'd go to Mom's brother, Uncle Brad, and his wife. And if they couldn't, Dad's sister Julie.

As I ate, I ticked off the list of aunts and uncles and cousins and family friends.

There would have to be some kind of worldwide major catastrophe before my sister and I had to even worry about foster care.

Roona didn't have that.

There was no Plan B if her mom couldn't take care of her. And her mom couldn't take care of her now.

Would Miss Oberman take Roona in?

She seemed like a nice person. She'd probably

been a teacher for about a hundred years, so she must like kids.

A new plan started to form in my head. A Plan B for Roona.

*T*he next morning, Harper was practically busting-out-of-her-skin excited for her playdate with Isabella. They were going to the park, even though it was about a thousand degrees outside, because it was Sunday and everything in Logandale except the grocery store was closed on Sunday, apparently. Even the gas station.

"Gideon, I think you should come with us," Mom said before they left. "It would make me more comfortable."

"I really don't want to." I settled back into the couch. Dad was at work, catching up on the day he missed to pick me up in Las Vegas. I felt bad, but it was perfect. I needed a few hours alone. "I'll just be here reading."

I held up my copy of *The Hobbit*, which I'd actually already finished.

Harper yanked on her arm. "Mama, let's go! Isabella is probably already there."

"Hang on." Mom kept her focus on me. "I want your word you won't go next door."

I stopped myself from rolling my eyes. It was tough. "I promise, Mom."

"We'll probably stop at the grocery store after the playdate. There's turkey in the fridge. Make a sandwich for lunch if you get hungry."

"Okay."

"Don't answer the phone. Unless it's me."

I wasn't allowed to have a cell phone, even though literally every kid I knew in Wildwood had one. She'd call the house phone, let it ring twice, hang up, then call back.

"I promise." I opened my book and started to read a random page, to prove that I was just going to go on an adventure with Bilbo Baggins while she was at Harper's playdate.

"Okay," she finally said. "We'll be back in two hours."

My heart thumped against my ribs as I listened

to them go out the front door. I listened harder until I heard the garage door open and the car back out of our driveway.

The clock on the living room wall slowly ticked away five minutes.

"I can't believe I'm doing this," I said out loud to the empty house.

I put on my tennis shoes, grabbed a bottle of water out of the fridge, then went out the back door.

The old folks' home was a straight shot, once I got on Logandale's main road. I pedaled as fast as I could, with an internal clock ticking down to two hours.

If Mom came home early, or if she tried to call, I was toast. Or if Dad left work early—which he could, since it wasn't a regular workday. Or if someone saw me and told Mom. I didn't know who. We barely knew anyone. But that didn't stop the fear from threatening to swallow me whole.

It took me about ten minutes to ride to the old folks' home, but it felt like an hour. I parked my bike, cursed myself for not remembering I'd need a lock, and said a quick prayer that no one would steal it.

I wouldn't be there long, anyway. Miss Oberman's truck wasn't in the parking lot. I needed to get inside and ask her mother how I could find her.

The problem was I was trapped outside by the keypad lock.

I paced back and forth, waiting with no patience at all for someone to come and unlock it.

It took awhile, but I got lucky. A man and woman about my parents' age came to the door with a couple of kids. I stood near my bike, trying not to look weird or suspicious.

The man opened the lock and herded his family in before going in himself.

I caught the door before it swung shut and followed them as closely as I dared. I stood near the two kids until the receptionist was caught up with signing the family into her big black book.

Then I took off down the hallway that led to room 115.

No one was crying today, at least. I didn't see any evidence of the Mean Reds, either. I was grateful for that as I walked fast toward Mrs. Oberman's room.

Her door was closed. Roona had just walked in last

time, but I couldn't make myself do it. What if she was sleeping? Or worse. What if she was dressing?

I knocked softly. When I didn't hear anything, I knocked again, louder.

An old woman's voice called, "Come on in, Theresa."

I opened the door. Clearly, I wasn't Theresa. Mrs. Oberman squinted at me from her wheelchair, parked near the window.

"Hello," I said, suddenly shy.

"Do I know you? I think you're in the wrong room."

"Um . . ." Now that I was here, I wasn't sure what to say. "I'm friends with Roona Mulroney? We visited you, you know, on your birthday."

"Roona," the old woman said. "Sweet girl. We haven't seen her in a while."

"That's why I'm here," I said. "I really need to find your daughter. Can you help me? Maybe give me her address?"

"Theresa? She—"

"Mother?"

I turned, startled. Miss Oberman, still old, but

not nearly as old as her mother, stood in the doorway. She looked at me with narrowed eyes and I wished I was just about anywhere else on Earth.

Not Boise, though. That helped me stand my ground.

"You're Roona's neighbor," Miss Oberman said. "Going to the middle school in the fall."

"Yes, ma'am." I shifted my weight from one foot to the other.

"Is Roona here?"

I shook my head.

"Is everything okay?" Miss Oberman sat on the edge of her mother's bed. "Is Miranda okay?"

She knew. For some reason that released the knot of tension in the center of my chest and everything came pouring out. "I don't think so. Roona says she has the Mean Reds and I'm not totally sure what that is, I've never seen *Breakfast at Tiffany's*, but I know it's not good. It's really not good."

"What happened?"

"She's baking all these pies. And cookies and fudge and stuff. And Roona's dad isn't in the air force. He's in *prison*." I covered my mouth with my hand.

"It's okay," Miss Oberman said. "I knew that already. Go on."

"We went to Las Vegas, me and Roona, to see him. Only we couldn't, because"—I waved my hand to encompass the whole prison thing—"well, you know."

"Who took you to Las Vegas?"

"We went by ourselves," I said. "On a bus."

Her eyebrows shot up and I thought it had probably been a long time since anyone surprised her. "Go on."

I thought about it for a moment. I had promised Roona that I wouldn't tell my parents, but I hadn't promised that I wouldn't tell Miss Oberman, so I did go on.

"Roona really needs help," I said. "I don't know how to help her."

"You can tell me," Miss Oberman said. "I've known Roona since she was a kid, her mother, too."

"Roona told me her mother grew up on a farm in Boise."

"She moved there when she was in sixth or seventh

214

grade," Miss Oberman said. "She moved back here after she married Roona's father."

"Roona's aunt Jane is coming to get her next week," I said. I was up against the wall of the truth. I'd have to either tell or walk away.

"To take her to the farm."

"Yes, ma'am."

Miss Oberman's face changed. "I knew Jane when she was younger, too."

My heart sunk into my belly. "Roona can't go to Boise."

"No," Miss Oberman said. "No, I don't guess she can."

I froze. She knew that, too. Maybe not the whole truth, but enough to not make me say out loud that Roona's aunt had hit her with a stick hard enough to leave scars.

"Can't she stay with you?" I asked. "I tried to talk my parents into letting her stay with us, but they think she's a bad influence. Only she's not. She really isn't. She's my friend—"

"You're a good friend, Gideon. I'm glad Roona has you."

"She doesn't know I'm here."

"No, she's not the kind of girl who would let someone do the asking for her, if she knew."

"I think her mom really needs help, too. Roona's afraid if she goes to Boise—"

Mrs. Oberman made a noise from her wheelchair. "Sad story, those two girls. Their father . . ."

I turned to look at her, confused. "Which two girls?"

"Miranda and Jane," Miss Oberman said. "Their father was . . . well, he wasn't a very good man. There wasn't a lot we could do in those days."

"You knew them, too, Mrs. Oberman?"

"Mother was a social worker," Miss Oberman said. "You should go on home now, Gideon. I'm glad you came here to talk to us."

I didn't know what to say to that. She was right. My internal countdown-to-Mom was still ticking away. I wasn't sure whether Miss Oberman was going to help, or what she was going to do if she did help. But I felt better for telling someone.

Roona was going to hate me if she found out.

Fifteen

I raced home, my brain scrambling for a reason I didn't answer the phone, in case Mom had tried to call. I thought I was probably okay, because if she'd tried and I hadn't answered, the car probably would have been in the garage.

It wasn't.

I ran around to the backyard, to get into the house through the kitchen. Out of habit, my eyes darted to Roona's yard. She wasn't in it.

What if her aunt showed up early?

What if Mrs. Mulroney had hurt herself or Roona?

What if Roona really did run off to try to break her father out of prison somehow?

I shook my head, hard. Was this what Mom lived with all the time? A thousand *what ifs* every time I wasn't in her sight?

I went inside and took a record-fast shower, so I could use that as an excuse if Mom asked why I didn't answer her call.

I wanted to go to Roona's, but I didn't. What was I going to tell her? That I'd told her secret to someone I barely knew?

*M*om called after I was out of the shower and lying on the couch pretending to watch *Terminator*. It was an old movie, but I'd seen it a bunch of times with Dad when Mom was off somewhere with Harper and it made me feel better to put it on, even if I couldn't focus on it.

"We're on our way home," she said. "How's everything there?"

What she meant was *did you go to Roona's?* Or maybe, *did Roona come over?* "Fine," I said. "Just sitting here all alone."

"I hope you're not watching cartoons," she said.

"I'm not." Not a lie.

"Can you take the ground turkey out of the freezer? I thought I'd make tacos tonight."

"Sure."

I hung up and went into the kitchen, found the meat in the freezer, and put it on the counter. Then I went back to doing absolutely nothing.

My brain was working, though. A million miles an hour.

I stayed there, thinking about Roona and her secrets and her problems, until I heard the garage door open. I clicked off the TV and sat up before Harper came barreling in.

"That was so *awesome!*" She ran in circles around the coffee table. "Isabella is my best friend, Giddy. I have a best friend, just like you and Roona."

"Gideon will make friends when school starts," Mom said as she put down her purse.

I looked up at her. "I took out the meat."

"Thanks, honey."

Harper plopped next to me on the sofa. "Want to watch *Finding Nemo*?"

I stood up. "Not right now."

* * *

The rest of the afternoon stretched on and on. Now that Mom was home, she wouldn't let me just bury myself in movies or television. Or video games.

She had a thing about screen time.

I sat at my desk with my notebook open to my plan, staring out my window.

I wanted Roona to come by. The more time that passed without her doing that, the deeper the dread sitting in the pit of my stomach buried itself.

I hadn't seen her all day. Not in her backyard. Not at my window. Nowhere.

Dad finally got home at six, and a few minutes later, he knocked on my door and said, "Hey, Boss."

"Hi, Dad."

"Dinner's just about ready."

I closed my notebook and slipped it into my desk drawer. I hoped it wasn't too obvious that I had something important in there. "Okay, thanks."

Dad came all the way into my room and sat on my bed. "How was your day?"

I turned in my chair to face him. "It was okay."

"You know," he said as he loosened his tie. "Mom will forgive Roona."

"It wasn't all her fault," I said. "She didn't make me go."

"I know. Mom knows, too. She just worries about you."

"Roona's my friend," I said. "And she's our neighbor."

"I know it. I promise, just give it a while. A couple of weeks."

"I thought we were supposed to help our friends and neighbors."

Dad's mouth tightened and he stood up. "Five minutes till dinner."

*T*acos are Mom's specialty. And they never had any gluten to start with, so they were the same as they always had been.

I just couldn't eat much. My stomach was in knots. Mom was watching, though, so I forced down most of one.

"Isabella's birthday is in three weeks," Harper said. "I'm invited."

"That's great," Dad said.

"Oh my gosh, Giddy." My sister took a big bite of

her taco and chewed it before going on. "Do you think that Roona's mom will make Isabella's birthday cake?"

I was a little startled by the idea of Harper, or anyone else, eating a cake baked by Mrs. Mulroney in the state she was in now. "No."

"Well, she might."

"I don't think so."

Before Harper could argue anymore, someone knocked on our front door. If someone had taken a picture of us in that moment, it would probably have been funny. Everyone but me had food halfway to their mouths.

My heart clenched.

In New Jersey, people knocked on our door all the time. But not here. We didn't know anyone in Nevada except Roona and her mom, and if they were here, then something was wrong.

"What in the world?" Mom asked.

Dad put his taco down and stood up. When Harper did, too, he put a hand on her shoulder. "You stay here."

I turned in my seat and watched him go to the

door and open it. I saw blue and red lights flashing in front of our house and I stood up.

"Gideon," Mom said.

I followed Dad. The taco I'd managed to eat sat like a lead ball in the pit of my stomach as I stood behind him. Miss Oberman stood on our porch with her arm around Roona.

"Mr. Quinton?" Miss Oberman said. "My name is Theresa Oberman. I'm a friend of the Mulroneys."

Dad stayed where he was, blocking the opening in the door with his body so I could barely see Roona. "Is everything okay?" he asked.

"No." Miss Oberman tightened her arm around Roona. "But it will be."

"I don't think I understand." Dad sounded genuinely confused. He didn't know all of Roona's secrets the way I did.

"Roona's mother is very ill. I'd like to go with her to the hospital, but I don't think it's a good place for a little girl. She thought maybe she could stay with you for a couple of hours."

I held my breath as Dad looked over his shoulder

at Mom, who'd come up behind me with Harper. Mom reached for the door and opened it wider. "Of course," she said.

Roona closed her eyes and tears fell down her cheeks. Miss Oberman bent and whispered something in her ear, then pushed her gently into our house. Dad moved out of the way for her and she came right to me and wrapped her arms around my neck.

I wasn't sure what to do, so I just hugged her back.

Miss Oberman said, "If you'll give me your number, I'll call in an hour or so. I should know more then."

Roona held on tighter while the adults exchanged telephone numbers, and then Dad shut the front door.

"Are you hungry?" Mom asked. "We're having tacos for dinner."

Roona let me go and took a deep breath. "I'm not hungry. Thank you for letting me come over."

Mom reached for her, brushed her bangs from her forehead. Then she looked at me. "Why don't you take Roona to the living room and let her rest on the couch for a while, Gideon? She looks worn out."

"*Y*ou told Miss Oberman, didn't you?" Roona asked quietly when we were in the other room sitting side by side on the couch. I almost lied. The word *no* was literally on the tip of my tongue. But then she added, "Truth."

"I went to the old folks' home and found her."

"By yourself?"

"I told you I wouldn't tell my parents."

She looked at me for a long moment. "I showed them my back."

"Your mom, too?"

Her face scrunched and her breath caught, but she didn't start to cry. "She was so sad. Sadder than blueberry pie."

"She cried?" I asked.

"I thought I was going to drown." Roona wiped at her eyes with the back of her hand.

"Why was there an ambulance?"

Roona's face crumbled again. She shook her head

and took a deep breath. After she blew it out again, she said, "My mom needed it."

"Did she—" I didn't know how to finish that question. Hurt herself? Take too much medicine again? Try to hurt Roona?

"She was afraid she would." Roona picked at the edges of the blanket she was sitting on. "Miss Oberman was afraid she would."

"You don't have to go to Boise." Surely not now. Not after both Mrs. Mulroney and Miss Oberman saw her back. "Do you?"

She shook her head. "I'm staying with Miss Oberman until my mom is better."

I sat back into the couch, relieved. "That's good. That's real good, Roona."

"She said she'd ask about taking me to see my dad." She shrugged one shoulder. "If he wants to see me."

My mom walked into the living room just then. She had two bowls of ice cream in her hands. "It's not pie," she said. "But I thought maybe you could use a treat."

Epilogue

It would be a while before Roona told me more about what happened that night.

"Miss Oberman asked about my back," she said without looking at me. She'd already forgiven me for telling her secret, but guilt bit into me anyway. "I didn't know how she knew. I tried to say there wasn't anything wrong."

"But you showed her," I said.

"Mom got upset. She was angry at Miss Oberman for thinking that she'd let me get hurt." She hugged her knees to her chest. "She pulled my shirt up, to show that there weren't any marks."

But there were marks. "She saw them."

"She wasn't my mom anymore," Roona said. "I mean, she was. But she wasn't. Know what I mean?"

I didn't. My parents were always my parents. Quinton-ish. Normal. I'd never appreciated that before, but I did now.

"She started crying," Roona said. "She couldn't stop. She . . . she crawled under our kitchen table and curled up in a ball."

"That's when Miss Oberman called the hospital?"

Roona nodded. "She crawled right under the table with Mom and held her like she was a little girl."

I knew the rest. Miss Oberman brought Roona to our house and took Mrs. Mulroney to the hospital. She'd been there three weeks.

"Not forever, though," Roona said. "She's already getting better."

In the meantime, Roona was living with Miss Oberman in a little house about half a mile from ours.

I still wasn't allowed to cross the street with my bike, but sometimes I did anyway.

And when I did, I always felt like Bilbo Baggins on his way to an adventure. On one of those adventures, Roona talked about her dad. She still hadn't gone back to the prison at Nellis Air Force Base to see him, but she'd written him a letter, and she showed me a letter he sent her in return.

It only had three lines.

I've made so many mistakes and I don't know how to say I'm sorry after all this time.

I would like to see you, if you want to see me.

I love you.

The next day, Mom came into my room and said, "Why don't you call Roona and invite her and Miss Oberman over for dinner on Saturday night."

Unexpected tears stung the backs of my eyes. I stood up and hugged my mom, tight. She wrapped her arms around me and kissed the top of my head.

"Can I ride my bike over to invite them?" I asked. "Please? I'll be super careful."

Mom pulled away enough to look down at me. "You'll walk your bike across the street?"

I nodded, my heart skipping a beat. "I promise."

She took a deep breath and let it out slow. "Okay, then."

I pedaled over to see Roona. I kept my promise and walked across the street.

She was skating in front of Miss Oberman's house. She wore cutoff jeans and a T-shirt with purple polka dots, and her hair hung down her back in two neat braids, just like the first time I saw her. The day we moved to Logandale.

Except she wasn't wearing her swimsuit over her clothes. And there was no baby blanket around her neck like a cape. She looked up and waved, her long, skinny arms and legs flailing as she skated toward me.